BUR Burmeister, Jon.

The protector
conclusion

DATE		

THE
PROTECTOR CONCLUSION

THE PROTECTOR
CONCLUSION

Jon Burmeister

ST. MARTIN'S PRESS
NEW YORK

Printed in Great Britain

ISBN: 312 65222 4

Library of Congress Catalog Card Number: 76–62750

First published in the United States of America in 1977

For my wife Audrey
who egged me on

Author's Note

For the material in this book I have had to rely upon the diaries, memoirs and letters of certain people – many of them in 'high places' – of whom only some are named and quoted. The others are best left anonymous. To them all, though, go my thanks.

J.B.
Montreal

I

Lord John Willoughby was normally a tense and jumpy young man. After six frustrating months in an unseasonally wet and weeping Spain, the scream that struck him as he opened the apartment door nearly frightened the wits out of him.

'Mary? Mary!' He bellowed through the dark as the door swung shut behind him. The rain, the flight, his confusion at being back after so many months, and finally the fright that his sister had given him had all contributed to a state of incontinent ill humour. It was nothing new.

'Johnny!' A lamp came on, revealing a magnificence of antique décor; but the prize, the pearl of it all was a girl just rising to her feet, barefooted, long-skirted, peasant-bloused, beautiful. Pleased, but a little confused, checking the date on the little watch that rode on the underside of her wrist – 'You're a day early!'

'Somebody cancelled at Madrid.' He began to haul himself out of his raincoat with disobedient fingers that kept sliding off the buttons. 'Are we alone?'

'Yes.'

'Grief, I thought murder was being committed in here! Or do you scream to yourself in the dark for fun?'

'It was the telly.'

'God.' He let the raincoat fall in a slithering slump and moved out of the bounce-back of light to kiss his sister. But the act was nothing more than a gesture to sibling affection. There was no real love between them. But she had been his

7

only confidant in a world he had treated with great suspicion since the age of eight years, so that he had missed her and was pleased at the reunion, and showed it.

'Have you developed webbed feet yet, brother?' She regarded him with sardonic and really unsympathetic amusement.

'It's a wonder that I haven't. No one will ever believe me that it could have rained so long, so hard, and so consistently.'

'Would you go into withdrawal if I offered you a drink? It's wet, don't forget.'

'That kind of wetness I can always endure.' He slumped into a genuine bentwood rocking chair without consideration for its age and kneaded the inside corners of his eyes. It was the act of a man who often wore spectacles. 'You're a darling. Teachers, please. Large.'

She crossed the room to the ancient cabinet that contained the drinks, her bare feet silent on the Aubusson carpet. 'How was the flight?'

'Poor. The pilot appeared to be under the impression that he was flying a fighter.'

She chuckled. He had always been a nervous flier. Then her voice, hollow out of the depths of the cabinet as she poured. 'Is there much damage at the Hacienda?'

'Less than one would expect. Although I suppose the wine will be foul. Miguel sends his love.'

She examined these last four words for a barb. Finding none, she turned to consider his expression. It was equally without guile. Then she said quite primly, 'Thank you,' and returned with the drinks.

'Welcome home.'

'*Gracias.*' It was very nearly impossible for him to relax but he was warmed by her presence, the apartment's relaxing richness, and his pleasure at being back. Yet even now he found something to worry at like a teething puppy. 'I suppose you realize that Lomax will be furious? He said that I should

8

stay nine months to the day or he would have nothing more to do with me.' His face closed up, brave in the absence of the psychiatrist he was about to defame. 'Shall I tell you something? He can go to hell. If he were a contortionist . . .'

'Hush, brother.' She wagged a finger at him. 'You will forever rush your jumps. I telephoned Lomax the moment your cable arrived. He was very pleased and felt free to say that nine months was perhaps a little on the long side but he had only been trying to make assurance doubly sure.'

'Well! From him that really is a concession.' This was said with a small, relieved grin. He would never admit it, but he valued Lomax.

'He wants to see you on Thursday at eleven thirty. Please make a note of it.'

John complied, in a little diary he produced from the inside pocket of his jacket. In the process, his left cuff slipped back and he exposed, just behind the gold strap of his watch, the white scar that represented the very nearly successful attempt he had made on his own life some twelve months before.

The Willoughbys always took their first drink fast. This fact had arisen through a combination of the innate nervousness and the redoubtable livers with which generations of them had been endowed. John and Mary were no exception.

'While you're on your feet, do you mind?'

'Not really.' She returned to the cabinet with a grace that had once been deliberate but was now unconscious. It was aesthetically beautiful, this movement of her body, but also healthily sexy. The days of the rawboned clothes horse had long gone and Lady Mary, apart from being rich, beautiful and titled, was also one of the world's top models, jetting to New York and Paris with the *sangfroid* of a lesser mortal catching a bus or train.

'Thanks for all your letters.' He said this quite idly. 'It kept me in touch with this country's death-throes. Also in a lesser way, father's current misdemeanours. Why didn't you write in October, though?' This last with an inflection of curiosity.

9

'Didn't I?'

'No you didn't.'

'Oh. I didn't realize that.' Her auburn hair spun as she turned to look back at him. 'Were you inconsolable?'

'I was inconsolable anyway. Cheers, thanks. Look, I had a cheap transistor radio with me that broke. Father, as you know, won't allow telly at the Hacienda, so I was stuck with Miguel. The two of us used to quaff valdepenas while we listened to the clatter of the rain on the tiles. He gave me garbled versions of the "news", which were mainly to the effect that it was raining in Spain – my God. I got every milli- metre of it, drop by drop – but also tail ends, deliciously phrased, about this sceptred isle's parlous state. You know the Spanish sense of humour – it is very direct and unsubtle but they have never really liked us no matter what our ancestors did for them. As a nation we talked about "German arrog- ance" for years, but we haven't lacked it ourselves and the Spaniards haven't forgotten. They really relished the *bad* news. Strikes. Factories running at half pace. Uncompleted contracts that had been turned over to the French or to the Germans or to them. Lawlessness. The London Bobby being armed for the first time in history. A thing called Work Force, and Zed-Force which needs a little explanation because at this stage Miguel's media broke down or got drowned or something.'

He regarded her morosely, then fiddled with his eyes again, a sure sign of weariness. 'Coming into town I saw some strange things.'

'Strange things. Such as?' She hovered above him, her breath clouding the rim of her glass, her body moving uncon- sciously to a slow rhythm that was within herself.

'Porters at Heathrow wearing red armbands. Beastly, surly fellows. On the way in, black teenage kids looting a shop. There was one copper in sight and he was running as fast as he could in the opposite direction, squeaking into his radio.'

'Don't blame the copper. It is surprising that he was even there on his own. These days they go in twos. And he would have been calling for a squad of the people you mentioned, Zed-Force. They do the work the LMP now refuse to handle. Mostly ex-soldiers. Very tough. Goons in a way, but loyal and clever.' She shrugged. 'An unpleasant necessity. I believe that even the King approves.'

There was a bristling silence. John was deeply concerned. He came of England's ruling class. Most of the members of the present Cabinet had watched him grow up. The King knew him by his first name. Politics had always interested him greatly although he had always been almost jingoistically patriotic, expressing (somewhat ingenuously) a firm belief in government by Parliament.

It could have been for these reasons that he was bothered about the prevailing state of affairs. This, in turn, could have been an indication that his solitary sojourn abroad had done him some good.

His sister wondered about it. Certainly he was a different person from the apathetic and scruffy young man she had seen off at Heathrow some six months before, twiddling the cases that contained his prized guns as though he simply did not care what happened to them. The John Willoughby of that time had not cared a tinker's curse about anything except a morbid review of the events that had led him into therapeutic exile by the command of his psychiatrist, to mend his brutalized ego.

Now his movements were brisk. His colour was good. Although it had rained a great deal it had obviously not rained *all* the time and the hunting that he had managed to get in seemed to have restored him to a good level of physical fitness.

Which was why Mary, studying him with great care, wondered whether her brother's good-looking body still contained an ailing mind.

Which was why, when he asked her for another drink, she got it for him instead of telling him to get it himself the way she normally would now that he had settled; accepted his reference to the 'dreadful turmoil' of the months before he had left England – while privately detesting him for the ass she considered him to have made of himself and his family – and finally, when he confessed to being 'barbarously ignorant' of current affairs, she bridged his ignorance briefly and subtly instead of telling him to read his newspaper. In a nutshell, she was prepared both to give and take a great deal more than she would normally have done.

'Olde England has come out in a new crop of dragons. They are standard, factory-issue dragons. Very fierce. Militant. Bright red.'

'Except that nowadays you spell "dragon" U-N-I-O-N, don't you?'

'Quite right. The rest of the populace is afraid that the dragons are going to gobble them up. So far the dragons have been quarrelling amongst themselves but they have a Summit planned for next month when I am afraid they may reach accord.'

'What about St George? Where has he got to?'

'Oh, he's still living in the Palace of Westminster. But he has become very senile and ineffectual.'

'Are you telling me that Parliament – and by extension Goverment – no longer governs?'

'I am afraid so, Johnny. It has been going on for years. Whitehall governs. Parliament is a ritualistic sounding-board. "Government" is a nebulous word. The Cabinet has become a rubber stamp for Whitehall's decisions. It started in the Sixties and has worsened steadily ever since.'

He donned a pair of lightweight, gold-rimmed spectacles through which he stared at her. He had at first seemed hostile, yet now said in sudden concord, 'Yes. I heard this view – only a view, mind – put forward: that a core of Oxbridge Civil Service career men run the country. An élitist group. The Government of the day is first mesmerized, then frightened, and finally overwhelmed by the mass of bumf thrown at them. Isn't that the way it goes?'

'It does. It wouldn't be so bad if they "governed" well but they have not. In a technological world, the majority of these people have degrees in the Arts. They have made mistake after mistake, covering up with more and more bad legislation.'

'Doesn't the Government realize what is going on?'

'Johnny, all the governments have known. It was first mooted a long time ago. Both Richard Crossman and Barbara Castle, amongst others, made plain what was going on. But it has been more obvious recently. We've had three governments in three years – Labour, that short-lived Liberal thing and now Wilfred Tuttle's Tories. All three knew.'

'But why haven't these governments reasserted themselves?'

'And be left carrying the can for this sorry mess?'

'I thought Tuttle a highly competent old man.'

'That's the key word: *old*. Wilfred is seventy-two and in poor health. I think he wakes up every morning and wonders how and why he got involved. There is talk that he might not last much longer.'

'I would hate to see England go ... I mean, after the Summit, that's the way it will be, won't it? Our family is seven hundreds years old. We can't just—' he paused, though he could not bear to produce the word '—flee.'

'There have been one or two defections. Freddie, for example, has more or less abandoned Montrae and taken his lot to Canada. But as a class we're tough. And there is hope.'

He looked surprised. 'After all that? One would need a Cabinet of very strong strong-men and I doubt they exist.'

'Jack Steele exists,' she said quietly. 'Heard of him?'

'Oh. The chap who was nearly assassinated this morning? They were yelling the news around Heathrow but I didn't bother to buy a paper. He was damned lucky to get away with it.'

Mary Willoughby laughed. 'He knew all about it. The Security people rumbled the man and Steele offered himself as bait.'

13

'That was foolish of him.' John regarded her thoughtfully. 'An emissary from Moscow?'

'Oh, no! A lone wolf. Lunatic left nut-case. I suppose there was an *element* of danger but not much.'

'If the would-be assassin had been rumbled, couldn't he have been rounded up beforehand? Couldn't all the gore have been dispensed with?'

'Yes.'

'Then it was almost a . . . heartless thing to do.'

'Of course! There're a number of synonyms. Heartless. Callous. Ruthless. Steele is that way.' She saw the question forming on his lips. 'Things like that. They bring him into favour with the people. Have you met him?'

'No. Some sort of base army-wallah wasn't he?'

'Lieutenant-General, ex-Royal Artillery. Retired from the army last year and stood for Tuttle in what had been up till then a marginal seat. He won it with a majority of three thousand. Within six months he was Minister of Labour.'

He frowned. 'I remember that when I was in Spain, getting my news second-hand from Miguel, there were stories about him. Broke three very bad strikes but used underhand methods. That right?'

She shrugged. 'Nothing that can be proved. The Coalminer's leader, Martin Grubbs, hanged himself one wintry eve. Jack Steele settled the strike the next day with Grubb's successor. He got around the Railwaymen somehow too. There was talk of money passing. I don't know. As for the Dockworkers, that Watt Tyler, who has a big head and deliberately changed his name so that he could pose as a leader of the masses, was only Number Four in the Union. The top three got drunk one night, quarrelled, and shot each other full of holes. Can you see that happening in Britain? Then Steele broke Tyler's spirit completely.'

'He sounds like your definition of Zed-Force – an unpleasant necessity.'

'Oh, he's more than that. I've already told you that he's

14

brutal. He is also handsome, charming, charismatic and very clever. Quite a combination.'

'Whoever runs this country, it would still take a long time to put things right.'

'I agree. After taming the Unions the next step would be a complete redistribution of this country's wealth, at the moment in the hands of five per cent of the population. The situation is like the words of that old song – the rich getting rich and the poor getting poorer.'

'This man Steele. Do you know him?'

'I have met him. Dinner parties. Things like that.'

'I wish I'd had the same opportunity. He sounds interesting.'

She studied him with enigmatic care. 'Oh, you'll get it, all right. You're going to work for him.'

He literally goggled at her. 'Have you gone out of your mind?'

'No. Lomax told me that he wants to implement something he refers to dramatically as "Phase B". In other words you have loafed long enough, dear brother. Occupational therapy has arrived simultaneously with one of Steele's secretaries dying. I telephoned Jack and told him about you. He's very interested. In fact, you are lunching with him at his home in Belgravia on Friday.'

He had become suddenly agitated and angry. 'I'm not ready for work yet; I'm damned if I will!'

'Lomax thinks you are ready. So do I.'

He glared at her. 'I'm not being pushed around like a . . . a pawn. Damn it all, I'll go back to the Hacienda!'

'Using what for money? Apart from which it would be an awful waste of time. Miguel has his orders. You would be physically ejected.'

John Willoughby jumped up. He strode up to his sister and thrust his quivering face at hers. 'Put it plainly. *Are you blackmailing me?*'

Mary calmly retreated. 'Isn't that rather a harsh term for a

15

sister who is trying to land her brother a cushy job?'

'You don't understand! *I'm still ill!*' He fiddled around with aberrant hands and shakingly lit a cigarette.

'Rubbish! I don't think so and, more important, nor does Lomax.' She was also becoming angry – enough so to prod him on the chest. 'Listen to me, my proud friend. *You* chose to fall out with Father and lose your allowance, so it has been sister dear who has been supporting you for far too long. I believe that Lomax is right, and if it is the only way of making you co-operate, I propose turning off your financial tap. So work you must, willy-nilly, to satisfy those Catholic tastes of yours. And with unemployment at its highest in this country's history, you would be a thoroughgoing ass if you didn't take the opportunity of working for Steele.'

He rushed over to her cabinet and whisky gurgled into his glass. He had his back turned like a naughty child but after a while said huffily, still without looking at her, 'You and Lomax have conspired against me.'

Mary did not bother to answer, and instead went through to the flat's small kitchen and putting together a cold meal – some beef and salads – which she brought back and set on a small table. Then she spoke the first word in ten minutes. 'You'd better eat or you'll get drunk.'

His moods could change like the weather. Unsulky, smiling even, he came towards the table. 'What do you think I should wear on Friday when I lunch with Steele?'

II

'This chap Steele is a confounded nuisance.' Dawson, the Assistant Commissioner who headed 'C' Division of the London Metropolitan Police was a lean, chisel-featured man who liked to be considered to have *savoir-faire*. He was a dapper dresser to boot, so that when he looked peevish he even did that in an elegant and debonair sort of way. 'Everyone wants to kill him.' He had walked with Jack Steele out of Parliament that morning, which entitled him to some overstatement. He was still recovering.

'He's indestructible,' the man on the other side of the desk said reassuringly. 'Sort of chap who can go through a dozen infantry assaults and emerge unscathed with people dropping dead all round him.' The speaker was younger than Dawson, a chunky man quite conservatively dressed in slacks, sportscoat and tie. He had light brown hair, features that were regular rather than good looking, and surprisingly innocent blue eyes. These were misleading, as many a villain had found to his cost. Detective Inspector Kyle had shot three men in the course of his career, of whom two had not survived.

'I know what you *mean*, Ernie.' Dawson placed his chin on his clasped fingers and regarded Kyle broodingly. 'But the fact is that he is a mere human, and a bullet in his cerebellum is going to make him just as dead as it would you or me.'

'Well, there was no *need* to put on that performance this morning, although that naughty villain nearly fooled us by dressing up as a copper.' Kyle had been in charge of the snipers. 'Steele wanted it. I could have nobbled that kid yesterday. We knew everything about him.'

'I know, I know.' As the Assistant Commissioner looked out at darkened London, John Willoughby was having his isolated little world shattered by the ultimatum of his sister. 'It was a gory publicity stunt. Dangerous too, by God.' He shuddered briefly at the recollection. 'I'm not made of such stern stuff. But how it works! The people love him.' He produced a perfect Cockney accent. 'Jack's our bloke!'

Kyle nodded. 'High and low, he's got them. Who was that Guardsman who fired the first shot?'

'Captain Nigel Fox-Carrington of the Coldstreamers.'

'Ye Gods. Anyway, his name won't help him. He's going to be charged with carrying a firearm in public without a permit. That'll stop him farting in church.'

The two of them briefly sniggered. Then Dawson said, 'I quite approve. It doesn't do any harm to put one of those toffee-nosed idiots in his place every now and again. The lordly fellows regard themselves as nigh sacred, the voluntary-bodyguard section of the Cult of Steele. Nevertheless. Orders have come from on high' – he flicked his eyes towards the ceiling and crossed himself – 'from no less than the P.M., that Steele is to have more protection. *Round-the-clock* protection. *Bumper-to-bumper* protection. Give me some more metaphor.'

'Twin-toilet protection.'

Dawson laughed delightedly. 'Oh, that's rich. Because you're the chap who is going to have to share the seat, right there alongside him. What one might call bum-to-bum protection.'

'Why pick on me?'

'Don't look so indignant. It is because you're a fine-looking young chap who doesn't drop his aitches or use his dessert spoon for the soup.' His expression became serious. 'It's also because you're a good copper, Ernie.'

What Dawson couldn't accomplish by orders or threats he did by flattery. It was well-known in the Division that he was a likable creep and also that he had pets. Kyle was one of them, literally Dawson's blue-eyed boy, and it often made him uncomfortable.

'Thank you. When do you brief me and when do I move in?'

'Now. Tomorrow. Like a whisky while I fill you in?' He got up and slid aside the panelling that hid his little store, speaking while he poured. 'Steele has a house in Belgravia. Three stories. I am going to give you a floor-plan with which you must familiarize yourself. Rather good spot of grammar there, eh? Practised it before you came in. I would much have preferred to leave that old preposition hanging out there at the end the way I would have before I rose to glory. Cheers.'

'Skol. I would like to have a run-down on the staff.'

'I have files on all of them except one whom I'm going to mention to you in a minute.'

'The one who will take the place of Steele's recently-deceased secretary?'

'Good fellow! It's nice to know that you read your papers. You will also draw a Walther and fifty rounds of ammunition. That should be enough unless they attack in battalion strength.'

Kyle laughed. 'What about the fourth secretary?'

'Well, that's the point. Steele hasn't engaged anyone yet but I'm a snoopy sort of fellow and I have ascertained that Lord John Willoughby is earmarked for the job. He is lunching with Steele on Friday, so you'll be able to meet him. It's only an interview at this stage but what with Willoughby's connections and Steele's publicity-conscious proboscis he is bound to take the lad on.'

'The name rings a bell. I don't mean his breeding, I know very well that he's the son of the Duke of Narsham who's a bit potty. It's something else.'

'You're warm, you're warm. Go on!'

Kyle's brow wrinkled. 'Scandal. Papers were full of it.' His expression suddenly cleared. 'Got it! He was having a hell of an affair with Harriet Rutherford-Graham, the telly personality. She turned cold on him eventually and Willoughby tried to knock himself off.'

'Excellent. Rather . . . well, I suppose *square* sort of chap, really. Loves huntin' and shootin'. Can't see him going all Commie and putting a razor blade in the soap but you'll have to check him out just like the others.' He shrugged. 'Apart from what I've got you will simply have to use your discretion, Ernie.'

'Okay.' Kyle finished his drink and Dawson handed over six slim files. 'Your homework. Check in tomorrow at about six p.m.; Steele will be expecting you. Incidentally, he's a very likeable chap. Very charismatic. It's an overworked word but he is. My own opinion is that if Tuttle has to scuttle – hah-hah – our friend Jack should be the next P.M., but it's unlikely, he's very junior in the Cabinet. Nevertheless, one of those Iron Men. The newspapers like the term but I prefer Human Dynamo. They never switch off. They never fatigue. Where the average man might get a coronary thrombosis from stress, these types get them from boredom, like Lyndon Johnson way back.'

'How often do you want me to report?'

'Every day. I won't always be here but just feed your bulletin into the recorder.' Dawson paused. Kyle had already got to his feet but the Assistant Commissioner dallied. 'Ernie, all that has passed was the good news.' He got up reluctantly. 'There's a little that is bad.'

'I was wondering.'

'Zed-Force are putting in a man as well. Let us be perfectly honest and admit that we need them, times being what they are. I also concede that they are well led and competent, although none of us like their methods. But for the first time in the history of England there exist two official, separate groups of Peace Officers in London. There is a lot of professional jealousy and rivalry and the moment the squeal came from the P.M. – which was addressed to *us*, initially – they insisted on sharing the task.'

'Who are they using?' Kyle's eyes had gone narrow and hostile, which dispersed that innocent look. In fact he looked very nasty and dangerous at that moment, which was why he had been chosen in the first place.

'Charles Holland. I don't know him.'

'I do.' Kyle began to turn away, his broad shoulders taughtening the material of his sportscoat.

'Good or bad?'

'Oh, both. Highly competent. Cold as a fish. Must have been imported from Canada, because that's where he used to operate.'

'All of that's good, so far.' The Assistant Commissioner smiled. 'What's bad?'

Ernie Kyle turned away again. 'He's a professional killer. Night, Bill. Thanks for the drink.'

Dawson let him out. 'Pleasure.' He closed the door and then stood staring at it for several seconds.

The man who commanded Zed-Force had been christened Colin Campbell, although he was not a lineal descendant of the only real soldier that the Crimean War had produced. He was a ginger man, a Scot of course, erect and military, apparently constructed of whipcord and high-tensile steel. He wore the same uniform as his driver, which was basically British Army battledress with a black beret upon which was embroidered in scarlet a small 'Z'. And instead of the three chevrons on the driver's arm, Campbell had his Colonel's insignia.

He was never referred to by his name. These were his orders. He was sometimes called Colonel Sir, and sometimes Colonel and sometimes Sir, depending upon the rank of the addressor and the mood of his chief. And upon this particular night his mood was as black as his beret.

'Ah where are the bluidy fools?' His car – equally black – was parked up the mouth of an alleyway and pointed across at a shopfront, the plate glass of which had been smashed in so that what jagged remnants remained reared up like razor-sharp shark's teeth. Inside the darkened shop a torch glowed briefly, on and off.

'Amateurs,' his passenger said briefly. There was not much to be seen of him in the dull light except that he was middle-sized, lithely-built, relaxed. 'I can go in there and clean them up for you if you want, Sir.' The voice was sharply American-accented.

'There'll be no need, Mr Holland. I could do it myself.' Campbell clamped a brief but iron-like grip on the other man's thigh. 'Of course they are amateurs! We knew about this one well in advance, although its not always that way. I just wanted you to see how we work.' He strained a glance at his heavy wristwatch. 'The boys are running a little late, that's all. I canna understand it. Unexpected hold-ups. I suppose. This is not the old London, Mr Holland, I assure you.'

'I don't know London,' Holland said idly. He yawned, fished around and lit a cigarette.

'Ach, it was so different. These days, you can get held up and have the breeks pulled off you – literally, mon – outside the Hilton in Mayfair. In the old days the Bobbies didn't have weapons, just a nightstick, in the dirtiest parts of the East End.'

There came the sound of engines, ghosting at first, then roaring very loudly as the drivers began to accelerate. Two trucks swept into sight, converging upon one another, and screeched to a halt in front of the shop. A dozen men piled out of each but they looked more like creatures from outer space – riot-helmets, gas-masks, body-armour, and Sten-guns glinted in the low light. They swept into the darkened, ruined shop and disappeared except for the two drivers who crouched at their windows, machine-gun muzzles pointing death into the darkness.

Campbell had left his seat and come around to Holland's side of the car in a movement so oiled and snakelike that the Canadian was deeply impressed. He admired competence of this kind. 'Two minutes late. That's bad, but we've got them.' At this precise moment, Dawson was expounding to Kyle and John Willoughby was the recipient of his sister's bad news.

From the darkened store came the brief stutter of a gun, a shout, the sound of swearing. A black man clad in jeans, tattered shirt and gaping tennis shoes rushed through the hole in the glass and stopped as though he had slammed into an invisible wall as both truck drivers fired sharp, controlled bursts into him.

'Ah, my bonny boys!' Campbell exhorted.

The dead man slumped. Blood oozed down the slight slope of the sidewalk. Through the glass came more men, whites, Indians and West Africans, their hands clasped above their heads, the Martian men bulkily escorting them. The Zed-Force troopers dealt out blows indiscriminately with their gun-butts, and one man went sprawling across the dragon-teeth of the broken window, which impaled him so fiercely that a sliver showed up through the torn shirt on his back. His shrieking was drowned by Campbell's roar.

'Kill that man, ye addled fools!'

Another gun stuttered, this time a demonstration of support for euthanasia.

'That's better.' Campbell holstered his Webley. 'Thought I might have to do it myself for a wee while.' He considered the cowed group being crowded into the truck as a young lieutenant trotted across the street and saluted.

'Get the lot, Malcolm?'

'Everyone, Colonel Sir.' The youngster was puffing but pleased.

'Good lad. Now you make sure all that blood is washed off, d'ye hear?'

23

'Fine, Sir.'

'And take 'em to the Work Force camp out at Croydon. I don't want you boys wasting time with trials and fussy Magistrates. Book them in as convicted. Six months without the option, nothing suspended. I'll see to the papers.'

'Yessir!' Malcolm saluted, did a sharp about-turn and trotted away.

'Fine lads.' The Colonel came back to his door and boarded. He was now completely relaxed. 'I told you that you were going to see two things tonight, the direct and the indirect. That was the direct. Like it?'

'Very good.' Holland flicked his half-smoked butt out of the window. 'Very competent. I'll be proud to serve with you, Sir.'

Campbell was pleased but tried not to show it. 'Notice that not a soul stuck his nose through a window? That's a good sign too. The public are keeping out of things. I'm training London. It'll be a pretty place anon, the way it was.' His voice sharpened as he spoke to the driver. 'All right, Ian, lad, you know where to go, and we don't want to keep this gentleman waiting. Get you gone!'

The Sergeant nodded and the car boomed out of the alleyway and nosed left past the loading trucks. It sped through half-dark side streets, eventually pulling up outside a dilapidated three-storey building near the Portobello Road.

'A sorry place, but useful.' The Colonel dismissed his driver telling him to return in an hour, then led the way in athletic strides up a creaking staircase to the first floor. 'This building has crawled away to die, much like the business in it. It's half empty, for that matter.' He stopped at a door, produced keys, unlocked, and let Holland follow him into a room nearly empty except for a cupboard, a bed, a desk, a typewriter and a small moth-eaten carpet.

'Horrible but useful. Like a drink?' Dawson was pouring for Kyle at that precise moment.

'Thanks.' Holland watched while Colonel Sir opened the

24

cupboard and produced neat whisky and two tumblers. 'I like it straight.'

'That's the only way it should be drunk, Mr Holland.' Campbell smiled. 'I havna any "rocks" for you, but this is malt whisky and doesn't need them. Your good luck. Now come over to the window, I want you to see something for which' – he flicked a look at his watch – 'we're just in time. To fill you in, the Garment Workers Union is demonstrating to-night. They have been infiltrated to the extent that they are nearly pure Communist. They will be coming past this window. Mostly women, poor souls worked to the bone. But they are very tough and they have a few men to strengthen their ranks.' He sounded more pleased than sympathetic. 'Here they come!'

There was the sound of shouting, gradually gaining. From Holland's left a group of women with a sprinkling of men amongst them, came into sight along the street. There were signs everywhere, reading SCUTTLE TUTTLE! ROUT THE TORIES!, LET THE WORKERS RUN THIS COUNTRY!, and nearly every sign bore the unmistakeable Hammer and Sickle of Communism.

'Bloody bitches!' The 'poor souls' seemed to have raised his ire. 'Now look at this.'

From Holland's right another contingent pushed into view. They were smaller in number and there were more men amongst them, but they were just as militant. Their signs read, DONT BELIEVE A WORD OF IT!, STRIKE MEANS STARVE!, DO YOU WANT TO WORK FOR RUSSIA? and GIVE THE BLOKES A CHANCE – THEY'VE GOT JACK!

'Strike-breakers,' Holland murmured from the window.

'More or less, although they're not on strike as yet. Now watch our subtle British way of doing things.'

The two groups had reached cat-calling distance and halted there while they exchanged insults. The street was blocked on both on sides, so one or the other had to retreat but neither would. There were some moments of hiatus. Then a solitary half-brick hurtled through the air from the left-hand group, propelled by the hefty right arm of a Garment Workers lady with a mop of grey hair. It landed in the midst of the opposing mob and a young woman fell down with blood streaming from her forehead.

There were shrieks, cries, and roars of anger from the dissident factor. But more half-bricks sailed across the intervening space and someone else collapsed. Shouting erupted on both sides as the dissidents retaliated with any form of missile they could wrench loose.

'Ah, bonny!' breathed the Colonel. 'Isn't it beautiful? Things will be coming to a head, now, keep yer eyes peeled!'

Within the mass of the Garment Workers a shot banged out, its echoes rolling along the tight confines of the narrow, congested street. A girl on the dissident side screamed, clutched at her belly, and collapsed.

There were roars of concern on both sides. The Garment Workers, confused, shocked and at a loss, began to retreat. The dissidents followed suit, so that in a moment the street was clear except for the body of the girl.

'Hell, that was ugly,' Holland breathed. 'I didn't know you fellows had got that bad.'

Campbell was grinning with delight. 'Watch! Watch!'

In a minute the Garment Workers were just a confused noise in the distance, badly rattled by the overaction within their own group and trying to find the culprit. There was a short silence. Then, with a roar, four Bedford trucks came in from the right and screeched to a halt. They were packed with dissidents. The 'body' in the street got up, took off its wig, and climbed into one of the trucks, followed a moment later by a woman in full Unionist garb who came sprinting up from the left. She, too, removed a wig while killer and victim laughingly exchanged handshakes. Then the trucks rumbled into first gear and moved off, gone in the diminishing roar of their exhausts.

Campbell smiled at Holland. 'The direct and the indirect.

We'll have that Union in tatters over this incident.' He got the bottle and topped them up. 'Now, I've briefed you on your duties as from tomorrow. What I didna tell you was that the Security Branch are also putting a man in. Name of Kyle.'

'What's he like?' Holland displayed a certain amount of professional interest.

'Och, a ninny copper. The L.M.P. go so much by the book that they're hamstrung. That's why they needed us. And that's why I want to prove that we're better than they are.' He pointed a stern finger at Holland. 'If there is any danger to Steele, I want you in there first. And I don't want silly arrests and fiddling around for evidence. If there is any danger to Jack Steele, *I want a dead man, d'ya hear?*'

Holland sipped at his drink and then smiled. 'You'll get him.'

III

'Tell me about Spain.' Lomax punched the record button with a heavy spatulate forefinger and watched the reels revolve in their cassette. He was a heavy man of about forty-five, slumped forward in an ancient leather armchair, chin on hand, in the attitude of Rodin's Thinker.

'The ibex was standing dead still at three hundred yards. I was very uncomfortable lying on the wet pine needles. I was using the thirty-oh-six with the Weatherby scope. I could hear Miguel breathing beside me . . . rain . . . rain . . .'

'The ibex, Miguel,' Lomax coaxed gently.

'I took first pressure. In the moment that I fired a white blob blotted out the target and the ibex was gone. Miguel had lens paper in one hand. He said a rain-drop was about to run down the lens. He apologized. He said he was very sorry, He had thought he would have the time to remove it.'

'An unfortunate occurrence.'

'Lies. He deliberately spoiled my shot.'

'Why should he have done that? You're his friend. He's known you since you were a child.' Lomax twisted his head to look at the figure on the couch. The answer came slurringly.

'Miguel has been making love to my sister since she was seventeen. Eleven . . . months.'

'Years.'

'Eleven years. He spoiled my shot because he knows I disapprove.'

'Has he ever spoiled a shot before?'

There was a strange, reluctant pause. 'No.'

'Then why should he do so this time?'

'Because he . . . because he . . . knows I disapprove.' Lomax shook his head but the voice continued. 'I can't go back to the Hacienda. Miguel and the Guardia would eject me. I am being made to work.'

'You employ the word "made". What do you mean by that?'

'I am being made to work. Miguel and Mary and Father conspired to make me.'

'What is wrong with working? You've had secretarial training. You were very good, in fact.'

'I'm . . . not really so reluctant now. It's just that I resent the conspiracy.'

This time the older man nodded. 'Fair enough, John. But the fact is that it will be good for you to work. Are you looking forward to the chance of working for Mr Steele?'

'Yes. A very interesting man. He has fire in his eyes. Very brave. A patriot.'

'Good, good! Have you made any contact with Harriet Rutherford-Graham since you last saw me?'

'Bitch! Bitch!' John Willoughby came up on his elbow, eyes staring, the movement so sudden that even Lomax started. Then the young man lay back groaning. 'No, no, no!'

'You are going to bump into her. Simply accept the fact. But you're entitled to hate her if you want to. How is your father?'

'The ibex was an easy . . .'

'We're not talking about the ibex now. How is your father?'

'I haven't seen him. He's mad!'

'I think "eccentric" would be more apt. Have you any desire to see him?'

'Yes.'

'Why would you like to see him?'

'To ask him why he murdered my mother.'

Lomax shook his head in mild exasperation. 'You have no evidence. We've been through this many times. He would have you locked up. I think you should visit your father and make peace with him even if it is only a surface peace.'

A pause, definite reluctance showing. 'The police . . . the Chief Constable . . . Father's friend.'

Yet again the leonine head wagged. 'Let us get back to Mr Steele. Do you think that you will be capable of doing the work entrusted to you in a competent manner?'

'Yes. As long as . . .'

'As long as what?'

'As long as there is no stress.'

'You are trained. The work won't be hard. What stress are you talking about?'

'Other people. They might whisper behind my back.'

'We will treat that kind of thing when we come to it. Now,' Lomax sighed, 'you will lodge with Mary. Are you happy about that?'

'Oh yes! Mary is very kind to me.'

'But you said that she conspired against you.'

There was another one of the pauses which came whenever he had to make an admission or a concession. 'It was probably . . . well meant.'

Lomax was very pleased by this. Smilingly, he said, 'What would you do if I were to introduce you to an attractive and intelligent young girl?'

The reply came promptly. 'I would . . . tell her to piss off.'

Lomax actually laughed. He switched off the recorder, straightened gruntingly and went through to an adjoining office where he dialled a number. There was a pause while he drummed his fingers and stared at a Landseer on the far wall. He had never liked it and was always threatening to take it down. Then he said abruptly, 'Lomax. I've had a long session with him ending up with scopolamine. It works particularly well with him.' He sighed and got to the point. 'The time in Spain did him good. He is socially acceptable, bright, sometimes even cheerful. He is tremendously eager to work with Steele. In fact, the truth only really emerged under the influence of the scopolamine. Just how he will react is difficult to say, I will make a more positive decision after I have seen him next week.'

Then he put the telephone down abruptly, without farewell.

IV

Extracts from a lengthy letter written to the author by Mr Ernest Kyle, at the author's request, in which portions of Mr Kyle's diary are quoted. Ed.

I stood on the doorstep listening to the chimes fade away, reflecting cynically that it was typical of a copper's lot to find himself about to commence duty as wet-nurse to a Cabinet Minister.

I was a very cynical fellow in those days. In childhood my father had convinced me that all politicians were self-seekers with feet of clay, so that the fact of being personal body-guard to a man whose name was on the lips of the nation did not impress me at all. I liked being a copper and was prepared to do my job within the limits of my capabilities which consisted of nothing more than a copper's long suspicious nose, a reasonable intelligence, and the ability to draw the Walther and hit what I aimed at in three seconds. But my attitude towards my charge was purely that sooner or later he would show up as just another tub-thumper who was in it for what he could get.

I will confess nevertheless that I was interested in meeting Steele. I was not politically aware; I knew that the Unions were giving tremendous trouble and that the printed notes I received in salary were buying less and less. But I took a long (and extremely ignorant) view that everything would come right in due course. It always had, hadn't it? The crime rate would drop as soon as our money troubles stopped, helped along the way by the Draconian powers all the peace-keeping bodies of England had been given. It is amazing how the young can blind themselves. And the not-so-young too.

The door was opened by what appeared to be a sturdily-built orang-utan wearing fatigues and a frilly apron. And it wanted to be playful. 'Say the password!'

'Let me in,' I said 'or I'll have you in the West Kensington nick for the night. The bugs bite.' I was cold and cheerless.

'The copper!' my simian friend beamed. 'Well, thank God you're 'ere, such a right proper tizzy we've been in! Wringin' our 'ands and peepin fru the curtings, scared to go out . . .'

We muscled and bumped each other around the doorway although I was at somewhat of a disadvantage being three inches shorter and three stone lighter. When I thought I was about to be spilled back into the street the orang-utan suddenly laughed and draped a paw over my shoulders.

'Welcome, sir! Just testing you out as one might say.' I was not at all mollified by the explanation but without jamming the Walther into his midriff and demanding an apology it seemed best to play it his way. He turned out to be ex-Bombardier Tim Careless, one-time batman to Jack Steele during their army days and now major-domo of the Minister's household. I noted in my diary that night that

I received a very warm welcome from this big ape who likes to pretend that he has a dome of concrete. He may fool some of the people some of the time but if he really is a chimp then he is the only one I have ever come across who can brace a man on the doorstep and gauge his determination, intelligence and the weight of hardware he is carrying in one minute of fooling. He is aided and abetted by a sturdy young chap named Clarke who also has the movements of a trained soldier rather than a servitor. Then they introduced me to an ancient crone who was apparently once Nanny to S., and is called 'Gran' by everybody. She resembles a derelict haystack and muttered to herself over the pastry dough like one of the witches in Macbeth, but I jostled her and received for my pains a look of knife-like intelligence from under the grey thatch. S. must be very clever and much liked to get this kind of loyalty because these people are not hired goons . . .

One was due to appear, though. Careless showed me to an extremely comfortable and cosy room, mentioning that Mr Steele 'was still at St Stephen's,* won't be long, though', and while I was unpacking my few changes of clothes I heard the door chimes again and about ten minutes later Careless threw open my door and marched in with a bottle out of which he proceeded to help the two of us. He was nursing himself and very angry and somewhat pale-faced and it turned out that he had tried his same tricks on the next caller and been summarily kicked in the balls. Charles Holland had arrived.

My Zed-Force 'colleague' turned up shortly after me. A very tight-lipped Careless took me down and more or less tipped me into the library and we were obliged to introduce ourselves. A strange character, immaculate and well-spoken, extremely controlled . . . was reading 'Kidnapped' . . . rather old fashioned hair style, heavily pommaded, looked like a Professor at first glance until you see the cat curled underneath, tail twitching . . . these hit men are sometimes like this . . .

Holland and I had very little to say to each other. It was a clear case of mutual dislike. I insisted on an exchange of credentials in a ponderous and policemanish manner and was

---

*Because many hundreds of years ago Parliament was obliged to sit in the church of St Stephen, many Members and their associates refer to the Palace of Westminster by this name.

rather childishly pleased because I knew I had annoyed him. I then returned to my room and an hour later

was called down to meet Jack Steele. Quite a big chap, had changed into tweedy stuff by the time I arrived. Or perhaps he seems big. Laughs like a smithy with the bellows going full bore. Slate-grey hunter's eyes. Very charming, made me feel completely at home, as though I had voluntarily come along and joined the household. In fact, after ten minutes of intensive S., I had to remind myself that this was not the case. Strangely, he doesn't use nicknames or short-forms. Thus I am Ernest. For example, 'Ernest, you must decide on how to handle your wet-nurse routine but, my boy, don't get me feeling all claustrophobic.'

By my fourth day of 'service' I had got to know both Steele and his entourage very well. Steele himself was as many-sided as the facets of a diamond. It was on this day that young Lord John Willoughby was due to lunch with Steele who had woken up with a heavy head and a growly disposition. Instead of resting, the way many men would have, he announced his intention of going for a 'health run' and made me come with him in a rugby jersey borrowed from Jenkins, gym shorts and a pair of tennis shoes a size too large. I stuck the Walther into my underpants but it kept jabbing me in the groin, so I ran somewhat like a peg-legged pirate, red-faced and blowing, while we collected a Pied Piper's tail of dogs, children and errand-boys. My charge took it all in his stride, carrying on sallies with nannies who recognised him. 'Oy, that's Jack Steele!' one of them would call and Steele grinning, would retaliate 'Hello, girls, leave me be now, I'm keeping fit for the women of England!' a sally greeted with randy cheers.

When we got back he showered and held an 'audience' in his 'chambers' (those are his words, not mine, he was fond of archaic words and phrases). Stark naked after a needle shower, with massive privates, he was in fine fettle, full of *bonhomie* and barrack-room humour. Present were Mike Jenkins, who was number three on his string of secretaries (they were all male, he would not tolerate a woman on the grounds that 'when you need 'em most they stop reasoning and start emoting'), Bombardier Careless who was as close to the door as possible, for reasons I learned later, and myself.

First he discussed with Jenkins the text of a speech he had drafted and which he was going to deliver at the London School of Economics the following week. Jenkins read it out and Steele was unimpressed.

'They're going to murder me anyway,' he announced, 'but I might as well subside under the rotten eggs and tomatoes with dignity. That's terrible, Michael, but knock it up in rough form and I will work on it.' His eye lighted on the ex-Bombardier. 'Careless, you dog! What do you want?'

'It's about the lunch, sir.' Careless displayed massive issue dentures in what was intended to be a winning smile.

Steele did not even pause for thought. 'Smoked salmon for starters, followed by Lobster Thermidor. Serve a good hock with both courses.'

He pointed his bare backside at Jenkins while he gruntingly pulled on his socks. All the young secretary did was to adjust his spectacles slightly. 'This young Willoughby, Ernest. I've been talked into seeing him with a view to taking him on in place of poor Clarence and I will probably engage him as long as he isn't covered in multiple tics, although I'm no Lord-lover, goodness knows.' He straightened and padded over to his walk-in wardrobe and chose a shirt. 'The kid has a bad personal history. Attempted suicide. Fell out with his father a year ago and got his financial tap turned off. Now I personally feel that a man's private life is no concern of mine but what I want to know is, is he going to function? Or is he going to crack up on me when I need him most, like a bloody woman?'

'Being a policeman and not a psychiatrist,' I said, 'I can only quote from other sources and say that he appears to be

36

over his nervous problems. He is capable and energetic if he likes what he is doing. Politically, he rather ingenuously describes himself as a "true Democrat" and a firm believer in government by Parliament. Incidentally, his personal psychiatrist has cleared him as fit for work.'

Steele grunted. 'Sounds all right.' His eye lit on his major-domo, still looming in the doorway. 'Careless, what are you doing here, I thought we'd got rid of you, you horrible little man!'

'We 'aven't any 'ock, sir.' Careless edged towards the door 'But I've got a very nice Chablis . . .'

'Not a chance! Now go out and buy the hock or I'll have your guts for garters!'

Careless capered out, managing to escape Steele's shoes, which struck the door-jam as he fled. 'You can't have Thermidor without a hock!' Steele snarled while we roared with laughter. I had heard that, as he had risen in rank, so he had acquired six set menus from a famous chef for use when entertaining and was terrified of departing from them.

Coming back with his shoes, he grinned at me. 'You'd better change before you freeze to death, Ernest. I think I'm going to like you, you're a nice copper. Just make sure you frisk young Willoughby when he arrives, eh? Give him a quick one up the crutch, that'll humble him.' He clattered out an iron laugh and I went off to shower.

Even in the short time I had known him, I had found that Steele used these moments of barrack-room brawling to shrug off the stress that was part of his daily life. I saw many other moods, though: there were times when he was grainy-faced and thunderous; sneering and abrasively wounding; randily drunk and demanding a woman; elegant, clever, a charming dinner guest; an impassioned, straight-talking orator; and last but not least the charming country gentleman who admitted a nervous-looking John Willoughby to his home an hour later, dismissing Careless with an imperious flick of the head.

37

I have given you my first few days in Steele's household in great detail in an endeavour to introduce you to a complex character. About the interview between Steele and Willoughby I know nothing, because guests were arriving and Steele took the young man away to his study, which led off the drawing-room. What I do know, though, is that when the two of them emerged twenty-five minutes later

I dislike using the word 'radiant' in relation to a male, but Willoughby seemed completely outside of himself. He was, so to speak, aglow, as though he had just *found* himself for the first time in his life. S. has clearly done some hard selling and the boy has taken it in. I also dislike using the word 'hero-worship', a sentiment found mainly in children, but I would say that from today, from the moment of that interview, John Willoughby will hero-worship S.

I wrote that within twelve hours of its happening and I think that the entry contains a note of surprise that Lord John Willoughby should be mesmerized by Steele's personality so quickly, but now in retrospect it is not at all difficult to see. This slightly-built, sensitive, lonely youngster, who was the next best thing to a nervous wreck, had met a man who was everything that he was not – well-built, endowed with the energy of a dynamo, humorous, charming and powerful. If Steele's magic could work on me so quickly that after two days I regarded myself as a member of the household, then it had to have far more effect on young Willoughby.

Unfortunately.

V

When Steele brought John Willoughby back into the drawing-room, more guests had arrived. Steele said, with one heavy arm thrown over John's shoulders, 'Gentlemen, meet the latest member of our team! Give him a hand, chaps!'

There was a burst of laughter, cheering and clapping while Steele smilingly introduced John to the newcomers. First came a lithe man in Town clothes, introduced as Lieutenant-Colonel Phil Brixton, 'An old pal of mine from army days.' Brixton, John noticed, wore the Artillery tie, Then he was taken to a tough-looking young Guardsman, also in mufti, who turned out to be Captain Nigel Fox-Carrington, the man who had fired the first shot into the body of the subsequently riddled would-be assassin. He shook John's hand with gusto. 'I say, you're Mary's brother, aren't you? How frightfully nice. Lovely gel.' Steele led him on to the imposing bulk of Watt Tyler, whom John was astonished to find present. Was not Tyler Steele's enemy, a red-hot Union Czar, the man whose spirit had been broken by Steele, now his host? Yet Tyler seemed relaxed and cheerful, assuring John gravely that he 'never drank anything but beer'. Indeed, Careless seemed perpetually to be handing him another tankard.

Conversation was noisy and enthusiastic, hardly interrupted by the arrival of Charles Bingham-Pope, M.P., who was Steele's personal secretary. He was short, stout, beetroot-complexioned and friendly. 'Know your father, of course. And knew your mother too, before her death. That was a sad

39

business. How is Mary? Absolutely charming young person!'

At this stage a recorder played the strident notes of a bugle call, bringing about a burst of laughter from the military men because the call was 'Boots and Saddles' instead of 'Come to the Cookhouse Door'. Nevertheless the group moved towards the dining-room and John found himself next to Brixton.

'That Careless is an amusing card.' Brixton was smiling. He delayed a moment. 'I suppose you realise that was a cavalry call played by an artilleryman?'

'I gathered as much.' John had taken an instant liking – something unusual for him – to the lean officer. 'But why?'

Brixton tipped his cigarette into an ashtray. 'Because the Regiment in which he served, and in which his master served until he rose to higher rank, has a somewhat unique tradition. Do you mind a bit of history? You're not one of these anti-military chappies, eh?' The handsome healthy face topped by short-cut blond hair contained a pair of twinkling blue eyes.

'Oh no!' John said quickly, 'An ... an army ... controlled by Parliament is fine.'

'That's an unusual way of putting it!' Brixton laughed. 'I promise to keep the history lesson short. You may know that the Royal Regiment of Artillery was founded as late as 1715. Before that time the only professional artillerymen were Master Gunners attached to the Royal Household. When war came they drummed up a band of bombardiers. One of them – oh, a mere three hundred years or so ago – had a unique experience whereby he and his men were forcibly impressed into the cavalry for a matter of a few hours. I gather that he was frightened so witless that he never forgot it and was forever talking about it. When his grandson found himself in command of a company of the first regiment of professional artillerymen to exist in England, he made the use of certain cavalry terms compulsory. I think he did it quite cold-bloodedly, frankly, because it made his men feel that they were different from other gunners. To this day the 74th Regiment R.A. carries on the tradition – and they're manning missiles. Imagine sounding the "charge" to press the firing button of an I.C.B.M!' He laughed. 'No, I can assure you, it is not taken to those lengths, but traditions are good for soldiers. They work a sort of magic.'

John was vastly intrigued. As they walked through to lunch he asked, 'Who commands them now?'

'I do,' Brixton said firmly as he took his chair.

They seated themselves before mounds of smoked salmon garnished with parsley and wedges of lemon. Careless's burly assistant came by with a bottle of wine in each hand and, as the glasses were filled, conversation became relaxed and cheerful. John had been placed in a position of honour at the head of the table on Steele's left with Brixton next to him and Bingham-Pope opposite.

He was still fascinated by Brixton's story and the fact that the rugged officer actually commanded the regiment of artillerymen who used the language of horse soldiers.

'Where is your regiment stationed?' He noticed Bingham-Pope wince humorously and felt the blood rush to his face. 'Or should I not ask?'

Brixton winked. 'Well, you have, and seeing you are who you are I don't mind telling you confidentially that we're somewhere in the wilds of deeper Northumberland.'

John laughed, flushed and excited. And the Missiles – are they intercontinental? Drumheads, I think I have heard them called.'

'Oh, indeed!' Brixton developed a look of mischief. 'I knew before I came down that I would be meeting you, so partly as an exercise and partly for fun I had the lads train one battery on Spain in case you might like to knock out the Hacienda!' This last was said with an amused slyness which showed quite clearly that Brixton knew all about the rift between John and his father.

Steele joined in the laugh. 'When I can spare you some time off, you must pay Phil a visit; you will be impressed.'

'I would like that very much. Are they really as accurate as that? I mean could you *really* knock out the Estate?'

'Well, I wouldn't like to do it just to prove it,' Brixton said amidst more laughter. 'But for example: do you have a tennis court there?'

'Yes, there is one, although we don't play on it very much.'

Brixton's eyes gleamed. 'I could drop a Drumhead on the net if I wanted to.'

There was a brief, impressed silence. Then Steele nodded several times and said through a mouthful of salmon, 'Phil is exaggerating. Let us rather be entirely accurate and say that he could put it between the tramlines.'

There was more laughter and Tyler spilt beer. Clarke and Careless, moving with the efficiency but lack of finesse that clearly stamped them as trained soldiers rather than trained waiters, removed the empty salmon plates and served the Thermidor which was so delicately delicious that John found it hard to believe that Careless had prepared it entirely on his own.

'Cooks are born, not made,' Steele said when the meal was over and they were lingering over the coffee. 'It's even his hobby – has been for years. He didn't get much chance in the army but whenever he was on leave he took over the cooking from his old Mum. She's gone now, poor thing.' He stuck a cigar between his teeth and took his time lighting it. 'Well, young John, have you enjoyed yourself?'

'Very much so.' John was slightly drunk.

'This is the beer and skittles part. It is a break, and it is necessary. You will learn how necessary it is. It makes up for the times you wake at one in the morning grinding your teeth; when you are heckled by men you know are fools or activists and you have to keep your cool; when you are caught flat-footed at Question Time by a supplementary; or when it gets really dirty and you have to get in low under the other fellow's guard and go for his guts with the point of your knife.' He brooded a moment and added, 'That's not even British. We're not constructed that way. Yet times are such that we have to do it.' He seemed overcome by gloom, and heaved it off with a visible effort. 'Tomorrow is the Sabbath. See to your devotions. Be here on Monday, sharp at nine. Now say your farewells, laddy, we have things to do. It is nice to have had you.'

VI

The Prime Minister had fled to Chequers for the weekend. He was a thin, mousy-haired, friendly-looking old man with an oversize mouth that could lift up his smile to the lobes of his ears. In the old days it had also been able to twist into a ferine snarl, but no longer. Wilfred Tuttle was old, ill and spent.

He arrived with his wife, Betty, late on Friday evening, consumed several large whiskies and a half-bottle of Beaujolais and thereupon solved all of England's problems in a rapid ten-minute summing-up while the rubber mouth remained almost permanently in a crescent shape. His wife nodded gloomily in agreement with every point he made, knowing full well that to throw in all the ifs and buts that came to mind would only lead to a fight. Instead she waited until he had petered out, head nodding in front of the fire, armed herself with detoxicants, and led him off to bed by one big ear.

In the morning he had a heart attack. It was spelt, confided Mrs Tuttle to the doctor over the telephone in a confidential whisper, H-a-n-g-o-v-e-r, and on the strength of what she told him, the doctor morosely agreed, but felt obliged to drag himself out in freezing weather to examine the most important patient in Great Britain short of the King.

'You are going to live, Wilfred,' he said after a thorough examination. 'All that is wrong with you is a mild dose of alcoholic poisoning. You must try to ease off, your liver isn't what it was when you were twenty-five.' He went over to the window and stared out at the sleet through which he would have to drive home.

'My heart goes bumpity-bump,' Tuttle said plaintively. 'Do you call that a hangover?'

'No, not really. All hearts go bumpity-bump. It just happens that yours misses one every now and then. Perfectly harmless but a sure sign of stress. You also have duodenitis, for the same reason, and bronchitis because you smoke too much – for the same reason.'

Tuttle said twitchingly, 'You're building up to something.'

'Yes, I am, except that it is not for me to say it. I can only suggest it: remove the source of stress unless you want to come unstuck.'

The Prime Minister regarded his physician and friend with morbid fascination. 'You mean, die.'

The doctor shrugged. 'I won't argue the point.'

There was a long, long silence while the thin little figure in the oversize pyjamas stared into space. Then, with an infinite weariness that carried the sadness of realization that more than fifty years of public life was finally ended, Tuttle said. 'I must resign.'

The doctor crossed the room and placed a hand on the Prime Minister's shoulder. This was his friend of many years and his voice was strong with emotion. 'You have made the right decision, Wilfred.'

'Am I well enough to go out?' Tuttle seemed to have aged in the few minutes.

'Strictly speaking, yes. But I would prefer you to lie in today with the weather like this. In fact I am going to give you a sedative.'

Tuttle waved him away with a trembling hand. 'I have tranquillizers by the dozen. All shapes and sizes. You should know.' He smiled. 'Thank you, James.'

Ten minutes later Wilfred Tuttle was speaking on his red scrambler telephone to the King.

'When you kill,' Ernie Kyle said unpleasantly to Charles Holland, 'what do you use? Or should I say what do you prefer to use? Knife? Blackjack? Piano wire? Dynamite?' He was hovering over the Zed-Force man in the library while Steele did paper-work with Hansom and Jenkins in his study, and made no pretence of the fact that he was baiting the Canadian.

Holland sighed and closed *Kidnapped* while keeping one finger between the pages to mark his place. 'You're presuming. And presumptious. Who says I kill?'

Kyle blew smoke on the Canadian. 'Come off it. You're a hit man. You took contracts for F.L.Q. Campbell got you out here and ostensibly you're on the Zed-Force payroll and ostensibly you're Steele's bodyguard. But you don't guard people. You don't work that way. It's tedious, boring and underpaid. The way you operate, if you make two hits a year you collect enough to allow you to live in luxury and pretend to be a professor. I know all about you, you punk, I even know where you were born – in a railroad shack so small you could hear your Ma and Pa banging in the corner. You got delusions of grandeur at an early age and in your twenties your twisted brain decided that professional murder was a very easy form of income. You're a success. Congratulations. But I want you to understand that I don't accept your presence. You stink. To me as a copper you're on the other side of the fence. I've got files on everybody in this house and a lot of Steele's outside contacts. Now I've opened one on you. It's slim, but I'm building it.'

'Go ahead and build.' Holland had yellow eyes like the big cats, the nocturnal hunters. He had the same nature, too, which admirably suited his profession. 'This room isn't bugged, Kyle, because I've looked. I can see by the way you're dressed that you're not carrying a bug either.' He smiled. 'Do you see how much more I know? I'm way above your league, feller. So now I'm talking to you confidentially. I'm telling you that if I choose to kill I do it my way and entirely dependent on

46

the circumstances. Whether I am Jack Steele's Zed-Force bodyguard or whether I've taken out a contract on him is an interesting problem for *you* to solve. It'll keep you busy.'

The eyes flickered. The tiger, burning bright in the darkness of the night. 'Just a word of warning. Keep out of my way, feller. Walk wide of me or you might end up floating down the Thames one moonlit night.'

'I quite believe it. Now we know where we stand. But just remember one thing. I'm a genuine copper. You're nothing more than a representative of a very new force for which the public has nothing but antipathy. I could book you tonight. Campbell might get you out in a day or two. I could book you again as soon as you were released. Campbell and I could go through the same procedure for weeks until either Campbell or I were fired, but in the meantime you would have a helluva fleabitten life in Brixton.' Kyle took a deep breath to control his suddenly mounting anger. 'This doesn't amount to floating down the Thames but in a way, for a person like you, it would be worse. So walk wide of me, too, Holland.'

Red murder showed for a moment in the Canadian's eyes. It was only a flash, and Kyle recognised it only because he was a policeman. Then Holland sighed and opened his book and said casually, 'Won't you go? I have arrived at a very exciting point.'

Henry Willoughby, Seventh Duke of Narsham, was standing at the number eight station on his skeet range with the butt of his under-and-over against his right hip, facing the High Tower. Leaning slightly forward, knees bent, eyes narrowed beneath bushy brows, he looked as though he were waiting for a tiger to smash out of the bamboo, an anticipation he had experienced on several occasions in his younger days. Now the only tigers to be found were in zoos.

He called abruptly, 'Pull!' and a clay pigeon hurtled out of the Tower at sixty miles an hour, head-on and straight overhead. It had to cover only twenty-six feet to reach him, but in

47

that fraction of a second the Duke of Narsham put his shotgun to his shoulder and fired and the 'bird' powdered under the full impact of pellets which had hardly begun to spread.

He about-faced to the Low Tower, crouched again, called again, and shattered the second clay pigeon directly overhead with the same devastating accuracy.

'Henry does it again.' He broke his weapon and let the two empty cases pop out. Then with his gun still open he waddled off the course to the blonde girl muffled up in coat, slacks and scarf who stood clapping her gloved hands next to Frame, the gamekeeper, who was taking the leads off the electronic control box which operated the throwers.

The Duke pulled the wax plugs from his ears and threw them away. 'Where've you been, eh? You've just arrived. You and that young scoundwel Swanby haven't been scwewing again, have you?'

Swanby was the Duke's older son, the product of a marriage too short and disastrous to be described. Swanby was handsome, muscular, oversexed, and where a brain normally lies behind the frontal bone, Swanby had what might kindly be termed a vacuum. And although the sibling affection between John and Mary was thin, between the two of them and Swanby it simply did not exist. Normally they ignored him.

'Well done, Henry! That was a brilliant round!' His offensiveness might have been addressed to the leaden clouds overhead.

'It's purely a matter of concentwation.' The Duke absently handed his shotgun to the gamekeeper, pulled gloves from his pocket and tugged them on. 'I don't want to wob the poor fella of his fair share because he's got a lot to learn, but good God the lad's insatiable.' He looked down at the gamekeeper, who was trying to pretend that he was somewhere else. 'Thanks, Fwame.'

'A pleasure, Your Grace.' Frame rushed away with his box.

'John is on the 'phone.' The girl's name was Caroline. She had the face of a very beautiful angel and a superb figure. By

48

occupation she was a photographic model and movie actress, but that the magazines in which she appeared and the films in which she acted catered exclusively to the hard porn trade. Everything she could have done, she had done. There was nothing left in her but draining nymphomania, and after that, tedium. She was now twenty-two and the Duke was sixty-three.

'John? John who?' Henry demanded querulously. Next to her Nordic loveliness he looked like a fat and lecherous leprechaun.

'John Willoughby. Your son.'

'Then I was wight. If you've just come from the house, Swanby and you have been scwewing behind my back.'

'The telephone, Henry,' she said patiently.

He shot out his gloved hands and grabbed her viciously by the throat. Her face purpled and her eyes bulged but she was helpless in the vice-like grip. 'Has he or hasn't he?'

The head nodded. Henry relaxed his grip and Caroline sank to her knees, her shoulders heaving as she sucked air into her starved lungs.

'You must stop this fibbing, it's too awful. All I want are the facts. I don't *mind* the boy having a go.' He placed a booted foot on her shoulder, pushed quite gently, and she toppled over. 'See you for dwinks. Seven o' clock sharpish.' Then he waddled away towards the privet hedge that led into the bare winter garden and from there trotted lightly up the steps into the huge house. In his panelled study the handpiece was lying next to the telephone on the desk.

'Yes, John, my boy, what is it?' He listened for a moment. 'Next week? Yes, that sounds all wight. Make it Fwiday. Swanby can pick you up from the station. Is Mawy coming? Oh, I see. All wight, my boy, I will see you at about seven, then? We'll have some venison, Just one word of warning, though – if your intention is to tap me for a loan, wather not come.' He nodded several times. 'All wight, all wight. Goodbye.'

Henry replaced the receiver and took a cigar from the humidor on the desk, staring across at his Turner without really seeing it. Then he said out loud, 'Now why does that little madman want to see me?'

The King had for some time been under pressure to marry. Having no intention of giving up his carefree bachelor life, he had embarked rather cleverly upon a policy of 'official' girl friends. These ladies were very carefully chosen. Although always of provable Royal descent, they invariably came from contentedly unassuming country families ranging from Scandinavia to the Netherlands, who had neither the inclination nor oft the means to launch their daughters into the jet set Being forthright and honest, the King had always made the nature of the association clear from the beginning and had been pleased and surprised by the reaction. Never yet had he been landed with tears or recriminations. The girl would have the time of her life, while the bemused matchmakers of the Press laboured under the conviction that the young monarch was earnestly – albeit very choosily – endeavouring to find an 'unspoilt' mate amongst the Royals of Europe.

The latest of the chosen few was a certain Princess Henrietta who could muck out a cowshed with the best and often clonked around the palace in clogs. She had brought an aunt as titular chaperone, but they saw little of the old lady who spent her time apparently trying to eat herself to death.

The King had taken a liking to the big, blonde, amiable girl. She knew that she was a decoy like the others before her and, content with tours and country trips, usually conducted by an equerry, Major Tudhope, Princess Henrietta made no demands on him as he whooped it up elsewhere. Yet when she tapped casually at the door of the King's innermost holy of holies, a study to which even the staff were forbidden except for a once-a-week dust and vacuum, he made no comment while he watched her home to the fire.

She was sensibly dressed in slacks, a heavy wool jersey and, thank God, brogues, not clogs. And there she stood as the call from the Prime Minister came through.

'Bad news, huh?' She had gathered the gist of it from his replies. 'Meester Tuddle is old and sick. He wants an audience tomorrow, a *Sunday* of all days. I think he means to resign, ja?'

'Oh, I'm quite sure of it.' He said the words automatically while puzzledly scratching his head, then jerked back to look at her. 'How the devil did you guess? You're not even . . .'

'English?' She smiled at his embarrassment. 'Ja, bud I still godda head. Who are you going to pud in his place?'

'Oh, I suppose they'll ask for old Bobby. Lord Braisthwaite. He is next in line. Or possibly Percy Swindell. It will be between the two of them. They are both bumbling old party hacks who should have been put out to . . .'

'Why do you not tell them to choose General Steele?'

It was the second time for a Kingly double-take. 'What do you know about Steele?'

'The head has eyes.' He was also beginning to realize that it had a brain, too. 'I haf seen him on television. A very strong man.'

The King had become deeply absorbed, virtually thinking out loud. 'Steele is twenty years younger than the youngest of the rest. He is almost totally without experience.'

She laughed. 'So this inexperienced young man breaks three bad strikes. Strikes vich Mr Tuddle and the others couldn't break. Or you for dat matter, I'll bet.'

He coloured, nearly became angry, and then grinned 'All right. I will concede the point. Steele is capable. But a lot of people regard him as a sort of axeman, capable of very dirty dealings.'

'Sure.' She sniffed. 'Accept Lord Whatnot then. It is not my country. Bud answer me first vun qvestion. Bismarck was a gentleman, eh?'

'Yes of course he was but . . .

'So who sent the Emms telegram? Who made a nation out

of chaos? Here is your pound going to hell on a toboggan and your Unions out of hand and you talk about dirty dealings! You want *eisen und blut*, not table manners! You want a man who eats guts for breakfast!'

He stared at her in astonishment while she quivered back at him, her blue eyes crackling with emotion. Then he said softly, 'Well I'll be damned. No, don't go, Henrietta. The sun is over the yardarm. What would you like to drink?'

Mr Benjamin Pickles and his wife Maud had by some miracle managed to produce two normal children both of whom were happily married and successful. The fact that they had fled from home at the earliest opportunity not to return for even the most fleeting visit and lived respectively in British Columbia and a hydro-electric plant in the wilds of the Highlands may be some pointer to their normality. The third child had not been quite as lucky. Coddled and spoiled to the point of ruination since his birth late in his parents' lives, Emmett had inherited equal parts of their mutual lunacy. In fact, given the opportunity to get away, he would not have taken it on the simple basis that, as a neighbour put it, he was as cracked as they were.

All of which serves to explain why Emmett had died at the age of twenty-three as the result of – to quote the Inquest finding – 'multiple gunshot wounds'.

At midday on Sunday, while the King was pouring beer for Princess Henrietta, Benjamin was busy slamming the door on two Security Branch officers who had been quizzing him and his wife for the fourth time in as many days.

He returned to the parlour quivering, headed for the chipped and cigarette-scarred cupboard in which he kept his gin, then suddenly sidetracked, flung open the window and screamed, 'If there's anything more you want to know, 'phone Moscow!'

'Well done, Benjy,' crooned his wife over her knitting. It was a scarf. She always knitted scarves because, as she was wont to put it, she had never learned to turn corners. 'Give me a drink, dearest.'

'Coming up, love.' He was still panting. 'That was rather good, eh? ' 'Phone Moscow.' Perfectly innocent remark, neither criminal nor libellous. Perfect little stab under the ribs, eh? What d'you say?'

'Brilliant, Benjy.' She took the glass of orange gin, gulped, and sighed with satisfaction while her piggy eyes flashed around the overstuffed room. 'We're not bugged, are we?'

'Oh no, no, never! I never let them out of my sight. I'm a damn sight too smart for them. Do you want the list?'

'Yes!' she hissed. 'Show it to me, Benjy!'

He half finished his drink in one Herculean gulp. Then he went on his knees beneath the gin-cupboard and pulled away the sheet of grubby paper that had been taped to it's underside.

'Here.' He was topping the gin up while she read:

'Minister of Labour Jack Steele, 93 Montrose Place, Belgravia.

'Captain Nigel Fox-Carrington, Coldstream Guards.

'Sir Arnold Dawson, Assistant Commissioner 'C' Branch, New Scotland Yard.

'Detective Inspector Ernest Kyle, 'C' Branch, New Scotland Yard.

'Colonel Colin Campbell, Zed-Force.'

There were ten names in all. All of the men concerned had been involved in the death of their son in one way or another.

'You have done a marvellous job, Benjy,' she breathed. She slugged at her gin and half of it slipped out of her slack lips and spewed down the scarf. 'And you're going to kill them all?'

'They murdered Emmett, didn't they? Of course I'm going to kill them! Starting at the top and ending at the bottom. Our Comrades will rejoice at the destruction of key figures in the Fascist hierarchy.' In truth, the Communists had expelled Mr and Mrs Pickles from the party years before for 'instability'.

'Benjy, you're a darling. I'm dry, love, please fill me up. What are you going to use?'

'I have my ways and means,' announced Mr Pickles, heading for the cupboard. 'Leave it to me.'

VII

From Volume Three of Memoirs of a Minister, '*Dark Days*' *by Wilfred Tuttle, page 431.*

It was a miserable sort of day but it fitted my mood exactly. I must confess to a degree of emotion I had not experienced in many a year. During the long drive from Chequers – I had left Betty and the maid commencing the mammoth task of packing; although whoever got it, Bobby or Percy, would let us go at our leisure, the job had to start some time – I dwelt largely in the past, wondering at just exactly what point this country had taken the wrong road. I must confess I could not find it.

My mood worsened even more when, just as we approached London, I saw two vehicles pulled up on the verge. One was a Zed-Force armoured car and the other a gleaming Jaguar. There was a man crumpled on the grass and I have seen enough war to know that he was dead. Four more men with their hands on their heads were being led to the Zed-Force car by three grim-faced soldiers armed with sub-machine guns. I tapped on the panel and Summers switched on the intercom and said that he had just got it on the news, the men had robbed a bank in Islington and killed two people.

After this, a mood of really crushing despair descended on me. I tried to throw it off as we swept through the Palace gates and succeeded with difficulty, managing to appear reasonably cheerful as I was greeted by Bobby Tudhope who managed very delicately to convey the news that I would not, in his opinion, receive a very warm welcome but he did not have the time to tell me why.

Another surprise awaited me: I was not taken to the Audience Room I knew so well but to His Majesty's personal study, which I had heard of but never seen. It is a fairly small room with none of the trappings of an office except a small let-down desk.

His Majesty was standing before the fire with the Princess Henrietta. The cloud-blanketed sun was high and they were drinking punch. The Princess greeted me most sweetly and His Majesty offered me some of the punch which we drank while making what the Americans so aptly call small-talk. This was mostly between the Princess and me, as his Majesty seemed preoccupied and, for a normally humorous man, somewhat stern.

After five minutes Princess Henrietta excused herself on the grounds that she wanted to see 'how the Bourguignon was getting on.' When she left, His Majesty smiled for the first time and said, 'She really means that, you know. One of her hobbies is cooking.' Then he changed the subject abruptly and expressed himself concerned to hear that my health was not good.

I told him that it was my ill-health which had brought me to him. He said that he had guessed this and I told him that I must reluctantly tender my resignation on the advice of my physician. He accepted it with, as he put it, 'extreme regret at seeing the passing from public life of one of England's most well-liked statesmen'.

I managed to control my emotion so that he did not notice anything because he then asked me to recommend a successor. I said that it had to be between Percy Swindell or Bobby, and that the Cabinet would decide.

His Majesty looked out of the window at the sleety weather and then said suddenly. 'Do you not think General Steele

56

a more capable replacement especially in view of this country's state?'

I was genuinely dumbstruck for a moment. It took me quite some moments to recover from my confusion, but thereafter I tried delicately to explain the position in which I found myself, whereby it was virtually impossible to consider anyone other than the two I had mentioned. A peculiar five minutes ensued in which I found myself engaging in an argument with my Sovereign which was, although I would not like to use the word 'heated', certainly of an intense nature. His Majesty stressed that this was his 'advice' to me, and that he had thought long and hard upon the matter, but I in turn did not see how I could budge from the standpoint I had taken.

He said, 'It is Britain's good we must have in mind, not Party politics. You and I both know that General Steele is the man to take the reins but you are too stubborn to admit it.'

I did not reply to what I considered a rebuff, so that we ended up in an impasse. His Majesty repeated exactly what he had said in the beginning, striding up and down the study. When he stopped in his pacing, he faced me with his muscular arms akimbo, and hinted in words I could not possibly misconstrue that *if I did not appoint Steele he must consider abdicating!*

There was a news-stand on the corner two blocks away from Jack Steele's house and as a tardy John Willoughby hurried by he caught sight only of headlines: TUTTLE SCUTTLES! TUTTLE OUT, SWINDELL IN! P.M. RESIGNS! This one had a sub-heading: RUMOURS OF ROYAL DISAPPROVAL!

Clutching his brand new briefcase he rushed on, and within minutes was tapping on the door of his new employer's house. It was opened by the muscular Clarke who was wearing an apron and holding a braying vacuum-cleaner in one hand as though it were a toy.

'Morning, Sir! Welcome!' Clarke yelled over the din.

57

'Come in, Mr Jenkins is in the drawing-room.' He tucked the vacuum cleaner under his arm and took John's hat and hung it on a peg on the hallstand. John went on into the drawing-room where Jenkins was seated at a coffee table, on which were a foot-high pile of stacked envelopes.

Jenkins looked up and smiled. 'Hello, John! Do come in.'

He lit a cigarette. 'Just to fill you in, in case you might think that opening mail in the drawing-room is standard procedure for a Minister holding a highly important portfolio, the answer is that it is not. We have in fact three sets of fully-equipped offices – here upstairs, at Parliament, and finally of course at the Ministry. But the boss is essentially a home-bird and in any case he seems to function better here. All the offices have intercommunication in case of need and if he is working here at home he can get anyone on intercom at any time. He is an amazing manager, or organizer if you like, of labour. He cannot bear inefficiency and there was a little trouble when he first took office but the bumblers and loafers have all been transferred elsewhere so that he has beneath him a highly competent and well-trained staff. So he dishes out the work and will brook no errors. He is competent and has an almost Churchillian eye for detail. This country has never had a more efficient Minister in any Cabinet in its history.'

'I can believe that,' John said sincerely.

'It's true, anyway, whether you believe it or not. Now, Mondays are always hellish. Hansom goes to the Ministry, Bingham-Pope prepares himself for the House where the boss will join him later on, and you and I open the post. It is almost entirely personal mail. And we do it here because Clarke goes howling around with that vacuum cleaner, Careless goes slow because he's a Sunday night drinker, and Gran sulks. In any case this Monday morning drawing-room thing has become almost a tradition in the short time the boss has been a Minister. It's also a good thing because it allows informal discussion, tossing around of ideas and so on. Sometimes Hansom pops in, sometimes Bingham-Pope, sometimes both of them.'

Jenkins put his cigarette down in an ashtray. 'Lastly there is this constant fear of assassination. It sounds ridiculous in England but it exists and we have to face it, so the less we move around, the better. Here, come on, get stuck in. All you have to do is open the envelope, extract the contents, show it to me, and then I will explain which pile to put it on.'

It was exactly the right line to take with the shakily nervous John. Jenkins was a bright young man. He gave the appearance of being fragilely constructed, but it was deceptive. In his leisure hours he played stand-off half for London Welsh and had been known to bite people in the loose scrums.

He watched while John slit open a letter, his fingers shaking so much that he dropped the opener, wrenched the envelope the rest of the way, extracted it's contents and handed them to him.

'Look, old man, relax. You're going to be nothing more than a typist for weeks.' He studied the two-page letter John had handed him. 'Now this is from a nut-case. It is all abuse. So we put it on this pile which never even reaches the Boss. He trusts us to use our discretion. Funnily enough, these letters from lunies make him very angry. They're mostly anonymous and without an address, so there's nothing at which he can hit back.'

Ernie Kyle came sauntering in. John had not decided yet whether to like him or not because the policeman's cynicism was so patent. He had also made it quite clear that he was 'not going to kow-tow to the nobility'.

Kyle nodded civilly to John and said, 'Forgot you were starting today,' something which John did not believe for one moment. Then Kyle turned to Jenkins and said, 'Sorry to make a nuisance of myself, Mike, but as from now I've got to read all the sick letters.'

'Not at all.' Jenkins cut into another envelope. 'But what

about Holland? Do you swop, or do you do it together, or do you leave him out of it?'

Kyle's face changed completely. 'Put it this way. He knows that the mail has been delivered and that you are busy opening it, yet he is sitting in the library reading the Theory of Relativity. Another small item worth remembering is that if the nut-case is foolish enough to put his name to his letter, he would go straight into the Work Force camp at Croydon with a faked Jail Order for six months minimum, whereas we would investigate the bloke the way policemen used to, in the good old days of civilization.'

'Then Holland can go to hell,' Jenkins said categorically 'Pull up a chair.'

Kyle sat down. 'Where's the boss? And how did he take being given the brush-off by his own Party?'

'He's in his study with instructions not to be disturbed unless it's from the P.M. personally.' Jenkins put down his letter-opener. 'He is making light of the other business but going by the set of his jib I would say that he is not amused. He knows how those old dodderers work – it's rather like appointing a new Head of School. The senior Prefects get together and the boss doesn't stand a chance because he is a *junior* Prefect. Genuinely, it's as simple as that. And as stupid. My personal opinion is that he nursed an outside chance and feels a bit let down.'

'But he is the country's logical leader!' John broke in excitedly. 'Just Friday alone was enough to convince. I'm a compulsive diarist and I recorded those exact words on Friday night. Only General Steele can save this country!'

Jenkins said quietly, 'We all know that.' He opened another letter. 'Now this is a *fan* letter and the boss adores fan letters. It goes on this pile over here.' Abruptly he reverted to the original subject. 'When he interviewed you on Friday, did he give you any sort of run-down on our situation? He does it better than the Chancellor of the Exchequer.'

John lit a cigarette with trembling fingers. 'Yes, he did.'

He fiddled around for his glasses and Kyle immediately saw the scar on his wrist and knew precisely how it had got there. 'First . . . first he said I must heal the breach with my father. I . . . I don't mind. I think he is right. I'll try, anyway. Then he told me that this country had eight weeks to go before it collapsed and the Communists took over and after that I might find myself riding in the same tumbril as him.'

'You see?' Jenkins waved his hands. 'Would the Chancellor say that?' He chuckled. 'Of course the Chancellor dare not but that's beside the point.'

'He said to me that there was hope. I can remember his exact words. He said, "We hope to heal sick Britain. We have the faith, the right men, and the dedication. With God's help it can be done." '

Even Kyle was impressed, staring at the young man for some seconds after he had ceased speaking. Then he said, 'Eight weeks is one hell of a short time.'

Jenkins said abruptly, 'Well, we've got work to do. Come on, chaps.' He turned to John. 'As I said, you're going to be a typist for some weeks until you learn more. Hansom, Moore and I shared an office upstairs. It is fully equipped with typewriters, telephones and all the rest. I will show you later on.' He opened a letter, read quickly, and whistled. 'Now this is a nut-case to end all nut-cases. Have a look, Ernie.'

Kyle took the letter, scanned it's contents, and then produced something between a groan and a laugh. 'Oh God, it's old man Pickles again. "Beware the hand of doom!" it starts. No name and no address but we burgled some of his correspondence and know his handwriting. He's the father of last week's would-be assassin. He and his wife are lunatic left as well as alcoholics.'

'Potentially dangerous?'

'Oh, maybe there's a five per cent chance that they could cause trouble in some hamhanded, bungling way but it's doubtful. We have bugged their drinking den and you should hear the way they go on.'

Jenkins laughed. But John said seriously, 'Can you do that? Can you plant a bug in anyone's house without their knowledge ... just like that?' He snapped his fingers.

'Yes,' Kyle said, 'and if you don't believe me read the Police Act Amendment.'

'But it's not democratic! It's ... an invasion of privacy!'

'All right then,' Kyle said sarcastically, 'we'll remove it if you say so, my lord. But just say that this old fool were to lay his hands on a box of dynamite and blow some people up including himself, probably. May I lay that at your doorstep?'

Jenkins watched as John's face flamed. He cut crisply across what could develop into a row. Kyle was no more than amusedly baiting the young man but John had become disproportionately angry.

'Look here, John, Ernie is only playing the fool. Do you always shake like that?'

'Only when I'm nervous.' He hesitated. 'Starting a new job has ... well, I am a little shaky.'

'Then take a tranquillizer.' Jenkins wondered just how wise Steele had been in engaging what appeared to the tough, well-adjusted little Welshman as the next best thing to a nervous wreck.

Careless came in. He looked like hell. ' 'Phone for you, Mr Jenkins.'

'Damn. I don't know why we open the post downstairs. Put it through to the hall, Tim.'

'Yessir.' Careless walked out, calling over his shoulder, 'Tea and turkey sandwiches coming up in ten minutes.'

Jenkins followed him out and then Kyle placed the Pickles doom threat before John, said, 'Have a good read, my cigarettes have disappeared,' and sauntered out.

John waited until Kyle's broad back had disappeared into the hall, then slipped a tranquillizer out of his jacket pocket and succeeded with difficulty in getting it to slide down his dry throat. It was fifteen milligrams of Valium, which would send most people to sleep; all it did for him was to stop him shaking.

He busied himself for the next ten minutes opening letters and placing all of them before the place where Jenkins had been sitting so that the more experienced man could check them. He read them all and was impressed not so much at the amount of 'fan' mail Steele received as by the quality. People from all walks of life and of all ages wrote offering help of any sort, congratulating him on the breaking of the last strike, sympathizing with him over the attempt on his life. Abusive letters were few and far between and usually ridiculous. One, for example, was a piece of cheap paper with the word FASCIST PIG scrawled across it in block capitals. John humphed out loud and tossed it on to the pile of 'nut-case' letters for Kyle to examine. At that moment, the door leading into Steele's study opened so suddenly that John was startled, and a sandy-haired man in battledress with a black beret in hand and a swagger-stick tucked under one arm strode out. He glanced at John, said 'Morning, lad,' with a heavy Scottish burr and was gone. An engine roared outside, tyres squealed, and the engine note diminished.

John sat staring at the portion of empty hallway he could see, his letter opener clutched in one hand, trying to place that beaky nose and gimlet-eyed gaze. He could hear Jenkins's voice talking into the hall telephone but paid no attention. Then Careless came in bearing a giant tea-tray and put it down nearby.

'Who was that?' John asked him.

'Huh?' Careless showed the passage of a rough night. 'Who what?'

'The man who has just left General Steele's office. A man in Army uniform. Sandy hair. A Major or more.'

'Haven't a clue,' Careless said. 'Didn't know there was anyone in there.' He straightened and added with quiet pride. 'Try one of my turkey sandwiches, sir. They're the best in the world.' Then he creaked out.

John opened another letter slowly, as though debating something within himself. Then, coming to a decision, he jumped up and lightly tapped at Steele's door, which the military man had left slightly ajar. He heard a barked, 'Come in!' and entered in trepidation to see the Minister of Labour seated at the far end of his room behind a big four-square desk. Steele's expression was stern, but changed immediately upon identifying his visitor.

'Well, young John! Welcome, lad.' He got up and strode across the carpet, hand extended. 'You don't look as shaky as when I interviewed you in here on Friday.' He did not know that the Valium had done its work. 'I'm pleased, but you will still have first-day nerves, so take it easy. You will be given nothing onerous for some time, anyway.' The ruggedly handsome face showed nothing but friendliness. 'How are you, lad?' John gulped. He said nothing while Steele took his hand in both of his own and squeezed them. The personality of the man was such that physical contact with him was electrical. He felt a shock jolt through his body. Then he stammered out, 'I'm . . . fine Sir. I'm . . . very well.'

Steele's eyes changed. 'Are you sure? No more hangups, laddy?'

John shook his head dumbly. He wanted to say or do something but it would not come. Steele seemed to sense both the confusion and the devotion, and was affected by it. Where he might have said more he just slapped the younger man on the back and said, 'Good luck, John, I am sure you will enjoy working with us. Now I'm frightfully busy, so get back to Jenkins and lend a hand, eh? I might see you later.'

John stumbled out and shut the door, to find Jenkins back at the table and Kyle standing holding several letters in his hands. Jenkins said sharply, 'Didn't I tell you not to go in there?'

'I . . . I was introducing myself.' He sat down shakily.

'In future I will tell you when to introduce yourself, and when not,' Jenkins said angrily. 'Come on, now, get stuck into these letters, you've done very little.'

'I . . . have to go to the lavatory.' John rushed out of the room.

'Good grief!' Jenkins stared after him. 'And his psychiatrist cleared him as fit for work!'

'He is a highly complex mechanism,' Ernie Kyle said. 'He takes fifteen milligrams of Valium at least three times a day. That would have you and me snoring. Yet look at him.'

Jenkins stared up at the Special Branch man. 'How did you know that?'

'I found out.' Kyle smiled smugly. 'I'm a copper, don't forget. I know it just the way I know that three months ago you scored a try in the last minute of the game, got drunk, threw a chair through the window of Three Little Pigs, and made an inflammatory speech about the independence of Wales. You then punched a P.C. who tried to arrest you and finally bought your way out of trouble. It cost you two hundred quid in bribes and you drew the money from your savings account at the National Provincial Building Society.'

Jenkins had gone first red and then white. "Good God! If the boss were to know . . .'

Kyle laughed. 'I'm concerned only with security, and as far as that goes you're cleared. Just thought I'd let you know what a clever chap I am.'

Jenkins started to laugh too, and for a moment they roared. Then he got up and went to the tray. 'I'll be mother. And do have a turkey sandwich, they're glorious.'

Careless came in looking worried. 'Sir, I wonder if we shouldn't get a doctor?'

'Are you *that* bad?'

'No, no! I mean young Lord John, sir.'

'Why, what the devil is the matter, he went for a piddle!'

Careless shook his head. 'No, sir, he went to the toilet but he ain't piddling.'

'Well for God's sake what is he doing then?'

'Puking his flipping head off,' Careless said.

VIII

'I'm afraid I've had to go out,' Dawson's voice said mechanically over the telephone, 'so feed in your report, Ernie, it will be recorded and I shall study it tonight. If you want or need to see me please feel free to say so. I've had the copper's blues all day and can't pin it down to anything specific.'

Ernie Kyle was in a call-box in Kensington, where he had taken himself for a brisk constitutional. The hand which he had ungloved so that he could dial was freezing, so he donned the glove again while cuddling the receiver against his ear with a shoulder. 'Steele is still alive. I went with him to the house where he forced me to sit in the V.I.P. gallery where I was so far away that if anyone had had a dip at him I would probably have knocked off the P.M. and one or two Cabinet Ministers as well as the would-be assassin. This chap is very tough and his staff are devoted to him. Holland bothers me. He sits around and reads. Steele can't stand him. Willoughby started today, of course. Most peculiar chap. When he arrived he was visibly shaking. He appears to have far more depth to his political views than we thought. He flew off the handle about bugging being undemocratic. I think you should get me some more background on his university career before he dropped out. Anyway, just when I thought he had calmed down to about a foot off the ground, he made Jenkins angry for popping in to see the boss without permission. I know that the boss was very good to him, but almost immediately afterwards he rushed out and honked his head off in the toilet. Hang on, I'm going to light a cigarette.'

He lit one clumsily and went on. 'Careless is a Sunday-night drinker. His favourite pub is the Angel and Harp. You could get someone to listen in on him one evening to see how much he lets go. Personally, I don't think that he is a potential security risk. Over and out.'

He hung up and walked a hundred yards towards the cosy pink glow of a pub window, passing several blacked out shops and two that were locked and barred, with Court Bankruptcy Orders pasted to their doors. There were far fewer people about at this early time than even six months before.

Kyle got to the pub door, looked back, said out loud, 'Eight weeks is a hell of a short time,' and went inside.

The pub was reasonably well patronized. He went to the counter and ordered a pint of Worthington 'E' and sipped as three more men entered. They were all wearing heavy coats and had hard, brutish expressions. Kyle put his tankard down on the counter but held very tightly to the handle as the first of the men to enter came directly towards him and growled, ''Ere, why the 'ell did you trip me mate outside, eh?'

'I didn't,' Kyle said evenly.

'Of course he did!' The second man barged up. 'D'you think I'm blind? I'll bloody-well teach you a lesson!'

Kyle threw his beer into the red face. With a backhanded flip he hit the first thug on the temple with the heavy tankard, and without waiting to see him collapse, banged the tankard down heavily on the head of the man who was trying to get beer out of his eyes. From the third he collected a glancing punch on the cheek but it was too light to have any effect. Kyle pulled the man away from the counter by the lapels of his coat jerked him off balance, put a foot down between his legs and sank to the floor. The man sailed over Kyle, fetched up against the pub wall with a nasty-sounding thud, slid bonelessly to the floor and lay still.

Kyle looked at the three bodies and the gaping faces of the

67

patrons. He gave the barmaid a small card which he produced from his wallet and said, 'I'm a police officer. 'Phone that number and a Flying Squad car will be here in a minute or two. Thanks for the drink.'

Lomax, in his customary slumped-over posture, chin on hand, pressed the Record button and spoke to the still figure on the couch. 'How did the first day go, John?'

The figure stirred a little. 'All right. Kyle is a Fascist.'

'Kyle is the policeman, is he not? Why do you say that he is a Fascist?'

'Goon. Bugs people's . . . houses.' The voice was distinctly slurry. The scopolamine had done its work well.

'Did you see the General? Did you meet Steele?'

'Yes.'

'Tell me about it. Tell me everything.'

'He was . . . very nice.'

'Is that all? Nothing else? What was your very first reaction when you saw him?'

The figure moved a little. The legs scythed. 'I . . . liked him.'

'Certainly, but I want more than that. Come now, John!'

The legs scythed again. Sweat burst out on John Willoughby's face. 'Shock. Electric shock. Right through my body!'

'Good, good, that's quite likely, many people of tremendous faith have this effect on people of less conviction. But I want you to tell me what *you wanted to do* after this shock you have been telling me about.'

'I . . . I . . . No, no!'

'John, you're not co-operating. I know what you wanted to do but I want you to tell me first.'

Sweat now streamed down John Willoughby's face. He bared his clenched teeth. 'I . . . wanted to love him.'

'Of course you did! But how did you want to express your devotion? What physical act did you want to perform?'

The sweat spattered as his head flopped back and forth, his expression agonized. 'I . . . no . . .'

'John, you know me and trust me. Come.'

'I . . . wanted to kiss him.'

'The way you would kiss a girl?'

'. . . Yes! Yes yes yes!'

'That's perfectly understandable, my boy. Every man and woman on earth nurtures a certain amount of latent homosexual instinct. Would you be prepared to go through a homosexual act with General Steele?'

'No! No no no! Never! I vomited!'

'Good. Good, my boy. That means you repressed it. Now relax. I will not ask you any more questions that will trouble you. Go to sleep.'

The figure went slack. Lomax studied John Willoughby for a moment and then went through to his other office where he sat down and glared at the Landseer, then dialled the same number he had dialled during John's previous visit.

When the receiver was picked up at the other end he said dryly, 'For a layman, your predictions have been remarkable. The homosexual desire has appeared and been repressed. He's ready.'

Then he put down the telephone.

'Mary?' John Willoughby called harshly through the half-dark apartment. 'Mary, damn it, are you here?' Then in the low light he saw the blurred square of white propped upright on the dining table at the far end of the room.

'Oh blast!' He remembered nothing of that part of the consultation with Lomax which had been conducted under the influence of scopolamine, the effects of which had worn off long ago. He was in fact in rather a healthily excitable mood and had looked forward to telling his sister about his first day at work.

The card contained Mary's upright, somewhat illegible handwriting: *Dearest Broth., have gone out on the Town.*

Hope the first day was not too taxing. There is a delicious Hotpot in the warming drawer created by my delicate hands amd despite your keen attentions there is still plenty of Teachers. Love, M.

John humphed and went through to the small but gleaming kitchen where he opened the warming drawer, examined the hotpot through the glass cover of the casserole dish, pulled a face, and returned to the lounge where he poured himself a large drink.

The whisky, of which he proposed to have several more, warmed him and relaxed him as far as was possible in a man as tense as he was. He wandered over to the sofa, intending to have an hour's read before he ate, and idly examined the magazines that Mary invariably left scattered on the cushions. There were *Vogue*, with Mary looking svelte and unbelievably beautiful on the cover, *Tatler*, *Illustrated London News*, and finally *Time*.

When he reached the small American magazine he froze.

The cover was a brilliant pen-and-ink sketch of Jack Steele, with a caption reading, STRONG-MAN STEELE OF ENGLAND. THE BRITISH DILEMMA.

John put his drink down and stared for long moments at the face he had seen in person that very day. Then he murmured something inaudible and began to flip the pages excitedly until he reached the section headed, *'Britain'*, which apart from the word was easily identifiable because there was another picture of Steele, a photograph this time, taken probably a few years before: Steele in battledress in some desert area, binoculars swinging from his thick neck, grinning and pointing, with a battery of field artillery and dunes forming the background. The caption underneath read, EX-WARRIOR STEELE and the story was headlined, THE LAST JOHN BULL. CAN HE DO IT?

London. Time's correspondent John Redmere writes: 'He has features as blunt as his manner, and the stiff-backed swagger of the regular soldier. His steel-grey eyes are about as inviting as a pair of bear-traps. When he speaks he bites his words off as though they were six-inch nails. This is Jack Steele, the ex-Artilleryman, now Minister of Labour in Prime Minister Wilfred Tuttle's shaky Tory government. Leaping into the world limelight by the breaking of three crippling strikes any one of which would, if it had succeeded, have seen his country floundering in a sea of economic distress, this hot-tempered son of an Essex farmer has been accused of accomplishing his task by devious means including violence, frame-ups and plain old blackmail. Says Steele in his brassy off-key voice (a voice very similar to the Oliver Cromwell he somewhat resembles) "I was asked to see what I could do. We could not grant the pay-increase demands because the money was not there. I found various ways and means, including straight talking amongst the rank and file, and of course one fell into my lap because three top Dock-worker Czars got drunk one night and shot each other.* I've heard the rumours that I had a hand in it and all I can say in reply is that this aspect has not been raised in the House, nor has any police officer been to see me, nor have any charges been preferred."

Asked how he went about his miracle-working, Steele said, "I started off by asking them how they would enjoy having their own personal estates bankrupted, because if we granted their wage demands this was one of the things that would inevitably happen to them. The money that we paid them would have no purchasing power. The rest is confidential."

Steele, the most junior in years and experience in a

*An obvious reference to Norton, Briggs and Lake who, in a wild melee using an old shotgun and two W.W.II rifles, shot it out fatally six weeks ago. (See *Time* January 7.) Inquest findings were that all three were heavily under the influence of alcohol at the time and had been bickering for weeks.

creaky-jointed Cabinet, is not always the hard-bitten soldier. He has several faces, all of them commanding, that reflect moods ranging from primal fury to a laugh that sounds like coal pouring into a scuttle. He is at his best playing the country gentleman because this is what he really is. He has many enemies but they seem far outnumbered by loyal-unto-death friends, and there is no doubt that he is brim full of leadership potential. Tory leader Tuttle's health has long been suspect and one wonders whether this dynamic man would be given the chance to lead his country if Tuttle bowed out.

Steele's only answer to this poser is a non-committal grunt and a growled, "I'm too low on the pecking order."

This may be so, given the Party's political structure. Nevertheless, with Britain on its death-bed, would not this modern-day Cromwell be wasted waiting in the wings, to be called onstage only when the final curtain comes down?'

John Willoughby found that his glass was empty and that he had been staring hypnotically at the last line of print for some time. In a daze he wandered to the cabinet, poured himself another drink, sat down and began to read the article all over again.

Charles Holland closed his book and glanced at his watch. It was nine o'clock and John Willoughby was at that moment commencing *Time*'s story for the second time. He lit a cigarette, staring across the library into space. He allowed himself only ten a day and had smoked eight. The ninth and tenth he always had with a drink, so after a moment he got up, pressed a buzzer near the door and resumed his seat.

In a minute Careless appeared, standing woodenly in the doorway. 'Yers?'

Holland's midnight cat-eyes showed yellow for a moment. 'Don't you mean "yes, sir?" '

Careless shifted his feet, contemplated what Holland had done to him when he arrived on Friday, and said tonelessly, 'Yes, sir.'

'Bring me four fingers of bourbon on the rocks.' Holland's words were clipped and precise.

Careless hesitated again, then swung about and disappeared, his boot-heels demonstrating his rage as he thumped away down the passage.

Holland smiled to himself while he puffed at his cigarette. He was a great believer in object lessons, and the one he had given Careless had been most effective.

He had become engrossed in his book once more when a voice at his side said, 'Your drink, sir.'

Holland closed the book. He was turning to look up, hand also reaching upward automatically, when his eyes changed and he began to move with blurring speed. But he was too late. He received three ounces of neat Bourbon in his eyes.

Whenever he fought, which was seldom, he fought with a feral ferocity for which he had trained for years. But he had been taken so off guard that he had no chance at all. While the fiery spirit still seared his eyes he was jerked savagely upright by his carefully combed and dressed hair. One arm was taken in a grip of iron and locked behind him and then his back exploded into a pain so blinding that he released a shrill, short scream.

He was in too much pain to fight, almost to stand. He sagged against his captor who said softly into his ear, 'Don't try it again, Holland. I've just torn your left trapezius muscle so badly that by dawn you'll have the worst headache of your life and will need physiotherapy for a week.' A hand slid smoothly within his jacket and removed the .357 short-barrelled Magnum he carried there in a shoulder holster.

'This is your last warning, Holland. I'm telling you just this time, and this time only, to *call off your dogs*.'

There was a moment of blackness and then he found himself lying on the carpet. His revolver, which he knew would by now be empty, hit him heavily on the chest.

'Goodnight, hit-man,' said Ernie Kyle, 'and sweet dreams.'

He switched the light off as he walked out and Holland, from his world of pain, heard Kyle whistling a lullaby as he went away.

It was 'Rock-a-bye Baby'.

Jack Steele was concluding his speech at London University, where he had been invited by the University Branch of the Young Conservatives. 'Britain', he said slowly, his hard steel-grey eyes seeming to pick out each individual in the packed hall, 'limps along like the caricature of the old man with gout. Factories run idle if they run at all. Of our three million unemployed, half are so by choice. The Draconian measures introduced by previous governments have met with little or no success because it is no use passing harsh laws for weak people. This nation has been struck by an epidemic of mass apathy. I can die from a common cold if I give in, and there lies the trouble. We are a nation with a mass death wish. But there is still time for the cure. All we need is the doctor who can produce the serum that kills the virus so that the man who is healed no longer says, 'I am a member of such-and-such a Trade Union, but instead says, "*I am British!*" '

The audience jumped to its feet as one, roaring their applause. The group on the stage behind Steele also rose and Bingham-Pope came forward and slapped him on the back. Red roses flew through the air to land on the stage. But the applause faded and finally died away as Steele raised his hands for silence.

'Ladies and gentlemen, amongst your overwhelming agreement with what I say, I heard a few cries of dissension. Let us hear from these people.' He pointed a finger like a gun at least halfway along the hall's length. 'You there, my friend, you were one of them. Let's hear you!'

74

There was laughter and more applause and 'Oos' of astonishment. For Steele to have picked out a detractor so far away displayed amazing powers of observation and a cool head.

A massive black man with an equally massive Afro hairstyle stood up, sweating and angry. 'I wanna tell you, man—'

'Your name, sir, I don't talk to faces, unless you're one of those who just wants a number because that's all you're going to have soon if we don't do something about it! Come on, lad, have you got a name?'

'Jake Jacoby,' the man said reluctantly while the audience were still laughing at Steele's previous sally. 'And I wanna tell you man—' he started to grow excited again, pointing a stabbing finger and beginning to babble, 'I wanna tell you that you're nothing but a Fascist pig, that's all you are!'

There was an uproar of booing and hands reached out to pull Jacoby down but Steele once again signalled for silence.

'Are you a student here?'

'I sure am! And I wanna tell you—'

'You've already told me. What is your age?'

Jacoby began to bluster, 'I don't see what that's got to do with . . .' but other voices called out, 'He's twenty-seven! He's twenty-seven!'

'Oh! You're taking one hell of a long time to get your degree, aren't you? One of those permanent students.' Steele came right forward to the very edge of the stage in brisk movements. His eyes narrowed into vicious slits. 'Jake Jacoby, I want to tell you this. You don't look like me. You don't talk like me. You are not a countryman of mine. You're not even my colour.' A slight, sly smile curved Steele's lips and his eyes roved the audience to see how this last would go down but there was only a deathly hush.

'Now I want to ask you something, Jake Jacoby.' He let the silence run. Then he suddenly slammed one heavy foot down on the stage so that it thundered and he shouted in a gravel-voiced roar, *'What the hell are you doing in my country?'*

The applause this time bordered on the hysterical.

Jacoby was somewhat disconsolately heading homewards towards his seedy lodgings when a black car pulled up suddenly next to him. He stopped, alarmed, with thoughts of Zed-Force tumbling through his head, when the driver leaned across, opened the passenger window and a familiar voice called, 'Hop in, young man, if you're anywhere near as thirsty as I am!'

'General Steele!' Jacoby's mind went blank. He did not know what to say and the strings of obscenities that he and his fellows normally resorted to seemed somehow pointless.

Steele's unmistakeable laugh clattered out. 'Not "General", for God's sake. Call me hey you or what's your name but not General, I'm a *civilian.* Now are you going to get in or do I break my neck craning in this position? I am going to a quiet pub for a quiet beer where you can shit me out to your heart's content and try and prove I'm a Fascist.'

Jacoby hesitated, studying the ruggedly handsome face. This could not be a trick, there wasn't another car in sight and he outweighed Steele by four stone. He said suddenly, 'You're on, man!' and laughed and got in. 'Winning me over won't work, if that's what's on your mind. And incidentally I hold a British Passport.'

Steele chuckled as he drove off. 'Giving people a go at political meetings and duelling with them in private are two different things. At a meeting, the gloves are off. There are no half-measures.'

'In a way you used me,' Jacoby said accusingly, lighting a cigarette.

'Of course I did. You played right into my hands. But I was using you for England's sake, not mine, so you shouldn't be resentful if you care.'

There was a long pause and then Jacoby said, 'I care. Sure

I care. But probably not in the same way that you do.'

'As long *as* you care.'

The big black boy said suddenly, 'That was quite a tough thing you did last week. I mean that assassination thing. Right or wrong, that needed a mile of guts, man. I admire tough men.'

Steele pulled up outside a pub. He switched off and put out his hand. 'Shake,' he said.

IX

On the second day, John Willoughby stared at the fourth page of *The Times* which contained a small picture of Colin Campbell. He studied the beaky nose and gimlet eyes and then he said softly, 'Why, that's him! Of course!'

He had been given a far fuller day, starting with an introduction to the offices at the Ministry and at Westminster Palace. Jenkins had been his guide and mentor although John thought he detected a certain hostility in the young man's manner that had not been present on the day before. John ably concealed this suspicion and asked the right questions at the right moments. After lunch Jenkins took him back to the house in Belgravia where they went upstairs to a large room fitted out with desks, typewriters, telephones, stationery and all the other impedimenta of a modern office. There Jenkins dictated upwards of twenty letters which were all of a personal nature and purported to come from Steele. They were, in effect, replies to 'fan' mail. They would be signed by Steele personally and had to be typed on Steele's personal notepaper.

Although the letters were short and simply phrased, John's rustiness and tension kept him busy until nightfall when he sighed and put the last of them aside. The work was faultlessly done but despite his personal problems the one thing nobody had ever accused him of was lack of brain.

Throughout the entire day three separate and totally divorced thoughts had occurred and recurred constantly:

Colin Campbell; the *Time* feature on Steele; and Jenkins's attitude. But John had done nothing about it and said nothing to anyone despite having bumped into Hansom and seen Kyle and Careless several times. Now a phone on his desk buzzed so suddenly that he jumped. Careless's hearty Cockney tones came over the line. 'Mr Steele's compliments, sir, and won't you come down for drinks. They're back early from the House.'

Excited and pleased, John hurried down the stairs into a gaining babble of voices all of which seemed to be talking at the same time. This was very nearly true, because Bingham-Pope, Jenkins, Watt Tyler, Fox-Carrington and several others whom John did not recognise were all telling each other of an hilarious incident in the House in which Steele had apparently put the Leader of the Opposition firmly in his place and made an ass of him to boot. Laughter rang loud and whisky and champagne – and Tyler's endless succession of tankards of beer – were circulating. Steele was in the middle of this friendly throng when he spotted John and called, 'Hello there, laddy, did they make you earn your keep today?'

John smiled and pushed forward to shake Steele's hand. 'Well done, sir, from what I've heard – and congratulations on that story in *Time*.'

Steele waved a hand and was drawn off. John found himself alone clutching a glass of whisky but in a moment he was spotted by the rubicund Hansom who was talking with Jenkins and Fox-Carrington. 'Come over here, young man. Have you heard the story?'

Out of politeness John said that he had only just come down from the office so Hansom told it once more and they roared with laughter. After this had simmered down, Hansom said on a more serious note. 'That was a frightful business in Soho. Did you hear about it? Bunch of beastly fellows cornered two Zed-Force chaps whose truck had broken down. Things were really looking ugly when another Zed-

Force vehicle arrived and the fellows really got stuck in.' His face went grave. 'Something like seven dead and umpteen wounded.'

Fox-Carrington said in a low voice, 'I wonder if that truck broke down accidentally or on purpose? Campbell is a wily bird. Just the sort of thing he'd do, eh?' He laughed. 'I'm prepared to bet that a lot of that bunch were on the wanted list.'

Hansom looked around and said, 'If I were you I'd keep that kind of thought to myself. Apart from which I can't say I approve of his methods, although they work. London is being cleaned up in no uncertain fashion.'

John said quickly, 'What sort of person is Campbell?'

Hansom shrugged. 'Reasonable enough. Highly efficient regular soldier. Wonderful leader of men. Extremely pleasant to talk to.'

'I . . . mean his . . . politics.' A little bead of sweat burst out on his upper lip and he licked it away.

'Good heavens, that's a peculiar question!' Hansom looked a little put out. 'How the devil do I know?' He squirmed uncomfortably, said, 'Tory probably, that kind of chap usually is,' and buried his nose in his glass.

'I . . . don't think so.' John gulped at his drink. 'I think he's a Fascist.'

Hansom's face re-emerged, positively startled. 'Long time since I heard that word! What makes you say such a thing?'

'The . . . things he does . . . rigging killings . . . taking the law into his own hands. It's not democratic!'

Hansom regarded John with concern. 'If I were you and I were looking for bogey-men, laddy, I would look to the Left. Do you know how we number our Communists? In millions. I'm dashed if I can tell you the exact number of Fascists, they're a dwindling breed since Moseley died, but it isn't more than ten thousand. They're regarded as a bunch of slogan-shouting idiots who dress up in funny uniforms on Sundays and get beaten up regularly.'

80

Kyle had arrived in time to join in the laugh. 'I don't think Lord John means it quite that way, in the form of registered, card-carrying members of the Fascist Party. I think he means that anyone who adopts undemocratic methods, who employs means that have not been thoroughly aired, vetted, debated, quarrelled over and finally passed by the Parliament of this country is a Fascist. Am I right, my lord?'

John had gone a dull red. 'I . . . yes, up to a point . . . there's more to it, of course. What Campbell does is wrong and the more people start following his example the more the . . . the whole structure of our principles of government is . . . being undermined.'

'Like my bugging of houses,' Kyle said with a grin. 'Now what we coppers should do is get a Bugging Act passed. Once that's through then to be thoroughly democratic a weekly list would be published featuring the names and addresses of people who are being bugged and the reasons. Thus: 'John Smith, 43 Green Street, suspected anarchist. Bug inserted in toilet. Is that right, sir?'

Both Hansom and Jenkins chuckled. John turned a dull, angry red. He said over-loudly, his voice gaining as he spoke, 'You are deliberately making me appear absurd but I don't care. What you are doing is *wrong!*'

Several men in the other group peered over and there was a momentary slackening in the conversation level.

Hansom said abruptly, 'Excuse me, I want to talk to Charlie over there,' and went off immediately followed by Fox-Carrington who did not bother to say anything.

Jenkins said very quietly, 'Take it easy, old man, you are making a frightful ass of yourself.'

Kyle tried to pour oil on troubled waters. 'I was only fooling.' He changed the subject. 'What was it I heard you say to the boss about a story in *Time*?'

John said sullenly, 'There was a brilliant profile on him, including an excellent cover picture, a pen-and-ink sketch. *Time*'s coverage is always excellent.' Then he turned abruptly

81

and walked out into the hall, turning in the direction of the stairs.

They stared after him. Kyle said, 'I take *Time*. Regularly. I don't recollect that issue.'

'Nor do I,' Jenkins said. 'I couldn't have missed it.'

'Then what is he talking about? Where did he see it? He couldn't possibly have got his magazines mixed up, could he?'

Kyle shook his head. 'He used the word twice, once to the boss and once to me. I think he must have invented it. His reaction to the boss was instant hero-worship, you know.'

Jenkins nodded. 'I saw that too. Odd sort of chap, isn't he?'

X

Mary Willoughby had draped herself carelessly on the sofa; she wore a turtleneck sweater, bleached jeans, socks and loafers, and the effect was magnificent.

'What ho, brother,' she smiled as John came in, tugging off his gloves and coat. 'We seem to be reduced to writing notes to one another. Either I'm asleep when you leave, or I'm out when you get back. I'm your sister Mary.'

John smiled. 'Drink?'

'Have you ever heard me say no?'

'On rare occasions.' He went to the cabinet, poured and returned with glasses.

'Thank you.' She flicked a glance at her watch which read the date as well as the time. 'This is your third day with Jack and I don't know a thing. What's it like?'

John sat down in the bentwood rocker, which he had adopted. 'Oh, it's all right. I'm still being shepherded and given the most footling jobs to do but the other chaps are so much more experienced.'

'First-day nerves gone?'

'I was nervous, yet somehow or other the first day was the best. I won't say that the job is beginning to pall – I'd be mad to say that after three days – but ... oh, I don't know. The Special Branch man, Kyle, seems to delight in needling me. He's a complete Establishment goon and I think he resents my title. Then one of the secretaries, Jenkins, has adopted a very hostile attitude towards me.

'Probably jealous,' she said.

He seemed relieved. 'That occurred to me too.'

'I wouldn't let the policeman bother me. That kind of brutish lout is always the same.'

'He's a lout, all right, although he's quite well spoken. Loves to adopt a superior, cynical attitude while behind it all he goes around bugging people's houses without their knowledge.'

Mary sipped her drink. 'Be careful with Steele, too, John. Watch him, a lot of these soldiers are self-seeking.'

'What on earth do you mean by that?' her brother demanded.

A strange bleakness in her had come and gone. 'Just what I said, but remember it. Anyhow, to the point. I have been thinking. Rare for me but I do it sometimes. Would you not like a small dinner for Jack Steele and three or four others? We could have it here. This kind of thing never does any harm, you know.'

'I think I would rather like that.' He warmed to the whisky. 'Bingham-Pope is a very nice fellow and Nigel Fox-Carrington says that he has met you.'

'Oh, Nigel! A typical Guardsman, isn't he. But very tough. One more, dear brother.'

'Is this for Saturday? If so, Lieutenant-Colonel Phil Brixton is coming to town. Usually pops in by helicopter. He's Jack Steele's very good friend, and a frightfully charming fellow.'

'All right. Go ahead and do the inviting.'

They made small-talk for another hour, had a light meal, then Mary, who was patently tired, excused herself and went to her room. She had had, so she said, an exhausting day with a particularly exacting photographer.

John sat smoking and brooding for a few minutes. Then he frowned, said out loud, 'Why not?' and went to the bookshelf and took down a copy of *Who's Who* which he knew Mary kept there.

He looked first for Bingham-Pope and gave a small 'Ah'

of satisfaction after reading the short entry. Doubtfully, wondering whether it would be there, he tried Hansom next and made the same sound when he found that not only was the man featured, but the entry contained the same information he had been seeking in Bingham-Pope's case. After he had returned the book he scribbled on a pad: 'Bingham-Pope, Major, Royal Marine Commandos, for 10 years. Hansom, Captain, Green Howards, 6 years.' He studied this for a minute and then added, out of his own knowledge, 'Careless, Bombardier, Royal Artillery, 21 years' and 'Clarke, Royal Artillery, 7 years.'

'Food for thought,' he said aloud, crumpled the paper into a ball and tossed it into the waste basket.

The London representative of *Time* magazine was called Hal Nathan and was inclined to be playful. 'It's wonderful to meet a genuine Special Branch man, I'm just sorry it's not me you're after, I'm a wild radical. Are you sure you wouldn't like to change your mind and arrest me? Just think, you'll be featured in *Time*.'

'I'll turn you over to Zed-Force,' Kyle grinned. 'You'll get six months without the option on a faked Jail Order.' He was satisfied that Nathan was not the kind of man who would abuse what amounted to a jocular confidence.

Nathan's expression had gone serious. 'We've been trying to expose those bastards since the thing in Soho but talk about a wall of silence.' He shrugged. 'Anyhow, that's my problem. Now Babs—she's my computer, I'm in love with her —has given me some dope that will interest you.' He opened a file on his desk. 'This magazine has reported Steele exactly seventeen times. He's an important figure and he gets a lot of coverage. These are photocopies of the stories. As you can see, none is very long and certainly cannot amount to a *profile*. And we *never* had him on the cover, pen-and-ink or any other medium. Is this guy positive about the cover?'

'Absolutely.' Kyle nodded. 'I went back to him, pretending

interest, and he told me he read the story about four times and studied the jacket for minutes. He can even remember the caption, if that's what you call it. It read, "Strong-man Steele of England. The British Dilemma".'

Nathan shook his head violently. 'No. No sir. Not a damn. Uh-uh. Can you think up any more negatives?'

'Thank you very much.' Kyle stood up. 'I appreciate the trouble you've gone to.'

'Pleasure.' They shook hands. 'Listen, newspapermen suffer from curiosity at psychosis level. What's it all about? Off the record. Promise. Boy Scout's Honour.'

'It's only one aspect of one person I have to keep an eye on, amongst many others. When he first raised the matter I was interested because I read *Time* regularly and I was sure he was wrong. But I had to make certain. Are you so sure about your facts that I must accept that he either invented it or imagined it?'

'Or dreamt it,' Nathan nodded. 'I dream stories sometimes especially if I've had a heavy night.'

Kyle laughed, thanked Nathan again and left the building. He went to the nearest call-box and dialled his Headquarters where he was put through to Dawson.

'I want,' he said slowly, 'to see Uncle.'

'Ooh.' Dawson was intrigued. 'In relation to which subject?'

'The twitchy one. The anti-bugging upholder of Democracy.'

'Thought so. Uncle's away at the moment but I can line it up for next week and give you the time and the date later? All right?'

'I hope so,' Kyle said, and rung off.

Extract from the Diary of Lord John Willoughby for Thursday, 6th March.

The completion of my fourth day in the service of Jack Steele. Reading my entries for the previous three, I find that on Monday I was quite heady with delight. Tuesday and

86

Wednesday are cheerful. Now, I am afraid, I must record certain unhappy doubts which will clash with my earlier happiness but this cannot be helped; my eyes have been opened and I must record what I see and think.

It started this morning when I wondered what had been bothering me since yesterday afternoon and it suddenly dawned on me that I had picked up an undercurrent in that house. Although it sounds melodramatic, all is not as it seems.

Now one cannot prove an undercurrent. The very word itself indicates that it is something below the surface. One cannot prove what one can only sense.

Yet it is there, and I think I detected it because I'd had experience of this type of thing in childhood, since the age of about eight. There too, was a constant undercurrent. Forget about the horrible rows I was forced to witness while Mary was away at school. Forget about Mother's drinking, where I was the medium employed to take liquor to her room in anything from Coke bottles to 4711 Cologne bottles. The undercurrent was something else. Here were two persons committing adultery in different ways – Father did it in London in a roaring drunk rumbustical Elizabethan sort of way with two or three wenches (as he called them) at a time, while Mother sneaked her lovers into her bedroom using me as the look-out. I will swear I was a better sentry than baboons are, from what I have read about baboons. But the point is that neither ever conceded their infidelity to the other, while both knew about it reciprocally. So the undercurrent was for ever present when they were together.

It is the same in the Steele household. I can smell it. It is so strong that I have been forced to do some thinking and have several whys and wherefores to record, none of which I can yet answer.

Thus:

1. Steele gave this country eight weeks to live, like a man with advanced terminal cancer. That is a dreadfully short

time. Yet in the same breath he says the patient can be cured. Surely only the most drastic methods – methods which I am unable to envisage – could bring about this miraculous metamorphosis in so short a time?

2. Why did Campbell visit him? Steele is the Minister of Labour, not War, nor is he the Home Secretary. He has no control whatsoever over Zed-Force. And it is alarming to consider that his visitor commands the loyalty of one thousand ruthlessly efficient and highly mobile troops.

3. Why is Steele perpetually surrounded by the military? His staff – with the exception of Jenkins whose background I do not know – are without exception ex-soldiers. In the case of his key assistants, they were high-ranking professionals. And there is Brixton who is perpetually calling. Nice fellow though he may be, he yet commands terrifying strike potential in his Drumheads.

4. Did not *Time* make an insinuation in its profile on Steele? *Why should he be kept waiting in the wings . . .?* The suggestion was possibly not ill-intentioned yet the innuendo is so strong it makes one wonder.

5. The Press has been full of the manner in which Steele made mincemeat of a heckler by the name of Jake Jacoby when he was addressing the Young Conservatives at L.U. What they don't know yet is that almost overnight Jacoby became a convert to the Cult of Steele and has split the Radicals right down the middle. I don't like those Reds, but Steele's underhand methods disturb me. Commenting on the incident (he was in one of his bawdy barrack-room moods), he said in that horrible off-key voice of his 'You know me. Old Jack saw Jacoby right.' And then he winked. What more can I infer from this behaviour than that money passed?

It follows from everything that I have said above that I have had to revise my opinion of Jack Steele. I no longer like and admire him, the way I did during those first few days. I detest falsity. And it would seem that there is a plot afoot. Yet

I have no proof. I would be reluctant to confide in anyone except possibly Mary, but I must first have evidence to substantiate my suspicions. For that matter, I say that I detect an undercurrent, that I do have suspicions, that a plot is afoot. But to what end? I am afraid that at this stage I do not know.

How sad that a man who promised so well should now cause shadows of doubt.

Charles Holland said to Colin Campbell. 'He got me from behind. I was relaxed, I was reading. He crippled me with a blow into this left back muscle, here.' He closed his eyes for a second while he kneaded. 'He told me in advance that I was going to have one helluva headache and need physiotherapy. I've got both. There is more to this guy than one realizes.'

'Holland.' Campbell got up from the chair in the seedy room from which they had watched the Garment Workers ladies débâcle. 'I have a lot on my plate. I thought that you were so experienced that you could eat Kyle for breakfast. You put your dogs on him without my permission and you got your just desserts. I'm nae sorry for you, laddy. It was a foolish move.'

Holland's headache, as predicted by Kyle, was so bad that he actually put his cupped hand on the top of his head while speaking. 'Things work differently in this country. But I'll tell you this. When I'm told that I am no longer needed to play watchdog for Steele, I'm putting my own contract on Kyle.'

'That's your business.' Campbell lit his pipe and puffed for a while. 'Things are peaceful there, I take it.'

'At the moment. It's a case of taking pulses. All of them – I suspect even Kyle is a recent convert – are devoted to Steele. That young Willoughby is different from the others, though.'

'Eh?' The son of a duke immediately interested Campbell. 'In what way?'

'He's a nervous wreck for a start. I'm not really tolerated there because Kyle gave them my background, but I see a lot from the sidelines and the shadows. Willoughby gets rattled easily and loses his temper at the drop of a hat. He is also stubborn and deeply suspicious. People are always talking behind his back, so he says. The others have got sick and tired of him, so he talks to me sometimes.'

Campbell frowned. 'That doesn't make him a security risk.'

'Not on it's own.' Holland moved towards the door. 'But in my profession if you want to stay alive you've got to be sensitive to the vibrations people give out. Vibes, they call it. Kyle is just a tough cop, tougher than I thought. He's a redoubtable enemy. Simple situation. But I get very bad vibes from that kid.'

'Meaning?'

'I'm not sure. I know that he's a great hunter. He's hunted all over the world. He's a gun nut. He loves guns, he loves talking ballistics, calibres, wild-cats, reloading. All that sort of thing.' He opened the door and raised his right hand in a flick of farewell. 'I've never met a gun-nut yet who wasn't a bit cracked. So long.'

Mr Benjamin Pickles poured two orange gins into chipped glasses, gave one to his wife, and winked. It was noon. At that moment John Willoughby, who had been reduced to enforced loafing at the Ministry, was asking Jenkins who had popped in for a moment whether or not he had served in the Territorials. Jenkins was preoccupied, and was by now also struggling to resist a desire to dislike thoroughly the other young man; he responded irritably, 'No, why on earth do you ask?' and John, caught at a loss, replied lamely, 'Oh, it's just that I never did military service and I'm envious of anyone who has.' Jenkins shook his head and walked out.

'What's that?' enquired Mrs Pickles with admiration. 'Looks awfully fearsome.'

Mr Pickles slobbered into his gin and emerged panting for breath. 'It's a double-barrelled shotgun.' He proudly exhibited the rusty old thing. 'Made by the Eastern Gun

Company in 1893 and just as deadly as when it was made. And these' – he heaved off the table a small but heavy box – 'are buckshot cartridges. Bought them today. They're Magnums, which means that they are very powerful indeed.'

'Who're they for?' she almost whispered.

'For the bloke on the top of the list. Here. You're empty. Let me fill your glass.' He scuttled away. 'Course, you realize the risk involved? I might not come back. Reminds me of what I've read about aeroplane pilots in the First World War. Going on dawn patrol, they would drink a toast the night before, and then throw their glasses over their shoulders.'

'Go on!'

At that moment Lieutenant-Colonel Phil Brixton, ensconced in deeper Northumberland, was talking to John Willoughby on the telephone. 'Just thought I'd confirm your kind invitation, old chap. I will be down and I will be able to come to dinner with you. Do please thank your sister, will you?'

John was very pleased. He liked Brixton. He stammered, 'Yes, yes . . . indeed I will . . . See you Saturday?'

'Saturday for sure. Do you remember that Jack suggested you come up here and look around?'

'Yes, I do, I'm greatly looking forward to the opportunity.'

'Well, it's been taken care of. You'll come back with me on Sunday morning. Doesn't matter if we've got hangovers, I don't do the flying. How does that sound?'

'Marvellous! I would like that very much!'

'Then consider it done,' said Brixton, and rang off.

Mr Benjamin Pickles's purple nose twitched. Tears came into his eyes. His voice quavered as he said, 'For Emmett!'

Maud Pickles lurched to her feet. 'For Emmett. When you gonna do it?'

'Sunday. He goes to Matins regularly at eleven. Cheers!'

'Cheers!' cried Maud. Then they drank their full glasses empty, hurled them over their shoulders, and smiled with satisfaction as they heard them smash on the floor behind them.

On Friday afternoon, with the rain bucketing down outside and the prospect of his visit to his father looming before him, John Willoughby left the Ministry offices in a state of trembling determination and returned by taxi to the house in Belgravia. Clarke let him in with a cheerful, 'Things gone quiet on you, eh, sir?' to which John replied, 'Yes, indeed, I seem to have been forgotten.' Clarke then disappeared into the bowels of the house and John mounted to the first floor, went into the three-man office and closed the door firmly behind him.

He was using the office purely as a base from which to plan and then act.

It was unlikely that the office itself contained anything of a confidential or even secret nature because it was seldom locked and the big, four-drawered filing cabinet stood open to anyone. Operating purely on the basis that it might give him a lead to something else, he lit a cigarette and began to go through it from A to Z while his mind worked rapidly ahead.

He was a hunter, and his hunter's instinct told him that whatever he sought would be contained in the massive wall safe in Jack Steele's study. Cracking it was out of the question and it had a combination lock. This was a depressing factor but he refused to allow himself to be affected by it. Secrecy, he insisted to himself, was difficult to maintain. Even men aware of the need for it constantly slipped up. With the knowledge that the root matter was locked away, they erred in minor ways. They made notes and forgot to destroy them, or they tossed them into the wastepaper basket. How many scandals had not come out of the trashcans of Whitehall and the White House until security had been tightened up?

John Willoughby was thinking along well fixed and logical lines. Even his almost ever-present tensive shake had disappeared, he was so engrossed. He was now in the same state as when he shot or hunted, completely in control of his normally rebellious body.

As he completed his study of the filing cabinet, which told him nothing more than that his employer was a wealthy man who kept his affairs in excellent order, he decided to start with Steele's study and move on to his living quarters.

He went down the stairs again contemplating with care the obvious fact that discovery in the study would put him in a very difficult position. It had been made clear to him by Jenkins that he was never to enter that room unless instructed to or invited in. He would have to hang everything on the defence of curiosity, and he was not at all happy about his prospects of being believed. Discovery in Steele's bedroom, on the other hand, could be laughed off apologetically as a natural interest in seeing how a very famous man lived his private life. Even then, there was an element of doubt. It would depend largely upon the identity of the discoverer.

The drumming of the rain obscured the slight noise of his footsteps on the hall carpet. He paused and looked about quickly. The old house was silent and the front rooms were clearly unoccupied. Moving with rapidity and decision, John crossed the drawing-room, opened the study door and let himself in, then closed it softly and firmly behind him.

He remembered the room well from Friday, when Steele had interviewed him there: thousands of books upon the shelves that lined the walls, a massive hearth in which an electric fire now blinked incongruously, scattered rugs, two or three easy chairs, a big four-square desk towards the far end.

John went straight to the desk. Apart from pens, telephones – one a red scrambler – a pipe-rack, an ashtray, a letter-knife and other such desk-clutter, there was a day-book for the current year.

John picked it up and began to turn its pages. He saw immediately that Steele used it as a memory-jogger more than anything else. Thus for the day before he had inscribed in his broad hand: 'Phone Walter,' and '11.30 P.W.'

He always used initials. As he paged, John failed to find any surname spelt in full. He learned very little from the entries except what he already knew, which was that Steele was an extremely competent and busy man.

The series of initials he found frustrating. When he saw an entry such as 'Charles to see H.P.' he could guess that the first man was probably Bingham-Pope but in not one single instance could he match a name with the initials.

At the end of the book, written on the last page, were a series of telephone numbers, linked yet again with initials. They had been there some time because the page was well-thumbed and John regarded them with surprise because there was a number finder on the desk, one of the type with an alphabetical key: when a given letter was pressed, the finder flew open at that place. By operating it several times he confirmed that it was in use, too, containing scores of numbers recorded not only in Steele's hand but two others which John guessed were those of Hansom and Jenkins.

John hesitated a moment, then copied the numbers and initials at the back of the day-book on to a piece of paper, shoved it into his pocket and then made a rapid but thorough examination of the only two drawers in the desk that were not locked. They held nothing for him, nor did the contents of the wastepaper basket.

It was a depressing moment. John moved towards the door, then stopped, considering. Finally he went back, grabbed a book from one of the shelves, opened the door and left the study.

He walked literally into Clarke's arms.

There was a moment of astonished silence. Then Clarke said aggressively, 'What the hell were you doing in there?'

'I . . . went to borrow a book.' He felt the shake begin to start and tried desperately to conceal it as he held up the leather-bound volume.

Clarke's expression changed but he said loudly, 'Sir, you know the rule. Please don't break it again.'

John's anger rose. 'I won't. And I completely forgot about

94

the rule. At the same time I don't think you should speak to me in such a manner, Clarke.'

The burly young man's eyebrows rose. 'Oh, so we're pulling our title, are we? Listen, your bloody Lordship, if you have any complaints make them to the boss.'

John said furiously, 'I certainly shall!' and stormed away. When he reached the hall something made him look back and he saw Clarke, hands on his hips, staring at him with a puzzled expression. Quickly, John turned away and headed for the office.

He spent twenty frustrating minutes there until he heard the front door bang and went to the window and saw Clarke pedalling along the street on a bicycle with a parcel container mounted ahead of the handlebars. The cheeky servitor was going shopping. With a sigh of relief and a glance at his watch, John headed for Steele's living quarters.

The passage was long and dark. The sound of rain was louder. He identified two guest bedrooms with a burst of light switches almost as quick as a camera flash, blinked his eyes and went on, finding a massive room on his left equipped with billiard table and small bar, hi-fi and television sets, easy leather chairs, old guns on the walls, a great hearth at the far end. A huge room, a den where men could relax and make man-talk. He absorbed it all in no more than five seconds, switched off once more, again held his eyes shut to adjust to the dark, and found himself left with one remaining doorway across the passage.

It was the master bedroom. The light was of low wattage and concealed, appearing to come from no particular point but just to glow redly.

His breathing quickened as he looked about. The room was huge and although the décor was masculine it was nevertheless resplendently luxurious. His feet made no sound on the carpet. In the middle stood a gigantic circular bed upon which two people would have seemed lost. The cover was gold with red tassels and the few chairs scattered about had the same motif.

John moved in slowly, realizing immediately that this was not just a bedroom but a room designed specifically for making love. He looked about quickly in jerky, nervous movements of his head like the very deer he had so often stalked.

On his right the wall was quilted for its entire length in a gold brocade, but on closer inspection two tiny red buttons intruded at different points. Padding silently, he crossed to the wall and pressed the first button. Immediately, a portion of the wall slid away with a slight hiss and revealed a brightly lit bathroom. There was a shower cubicle, wash-hand basin, toilet, and glass shelves containing shaving equipment, and the like. Although the walls were gleamingly tiled, the bathroom was functional and mundane compared with the bedroom itself.

John pressed the button again and the panel slid shut, the light going out in the same moment. He moved further along and pressed the second button.

The quilted wall slid aside and he was presented with a giant walk-in wardrobe. Steele's clothes hung on coat-hangers on two bars parallel to each other for the complete width of the wardrobe. John stared at a splendid array of suits, sports-jackets and casual clothes. Completely forgetting himself, momentarily lost in a world of sartorial splendour, he used his reasonable height to peer over the top of the first row to study the second. It was as richly hung as the first. A rather dapper dresser himself, his eyes ran down the rank of heavy, expensive clothes until they stopped suddenly at a hanger which obviously contained a suit or jacket of some sort, but which was covered in a black plastic cover impenetrable to the eye.

His curiosity was aroused. Puffing with nervous tension, he ducked under the first rail and emerged between the two, examined the cover and found a zip that ran down the back. He grabbed it with unsteady fingers and pulled it all the way down, then wrestled with the cover, pulling it aside and downwards until he had exposed what it contained.

It was a military dress uniform.

John stared at it in astonishment. It was the scarlet of England, magnificent with braid and epaulettes, and had clearly never been worn before. Its newness sparkled in the automatic light of the walk-in wardrobe. But what sparkled even more to John Willoughby's eyes were the insignia.

He knew little about the military, but only a fool would be unable to recognise the crossed batons of a Field Marshal.

He let out his breath in a long hissing sigh, staring at the insignia as though in horror. He whispered, *Field Marshal!* even while he heard the smothered cough from the stairs and fumblingly rushed the plastic cover back over the jacket, ran the zip up again, jumped under the rail and frantically pressed the red button on the outside of the quilted door. He fleetingly saw it slide shut as he dashed for the doorway light and plunged the whole area into darkness while Careless's voice, raw-edged with tension, came from the end of the passage.

'Hey! What's going on 'ere? Who's playing the bloody fool?'

Using the carpeting as his ally and moving in total darkness, John slipped from the doorway across the passage into the den. It was now fully dark but lightning tore a raw gap in it just as he gained the other room. The storm was directly over London and thunder boomed immediately.

He found the billiard table by feel, slid around it and crouched on the other side.

Careless came down the passage. John could not hear his feet but his voice jumped suddenly nearer. 'Oy! That's not you Mister Jenkins, playing the bloody fool?'

He remained silent. Careless's voice roughened. 'I'm sick and tired of this and I'm holding a bloody dirty great gun here. Whoever you are, there's nothing worth stealing that don't need a truck so come out quietly and it'll be the better for you!'

The subdued lighting in Steele's room came on. John even saw Careless's tough, blocky figure outlined against it for a second before he disappeared from view. He heard the panels of the bathroom and walk-in wardrobe slide open and shut.

Then Careless came out and entered the den.

'I smell you,' Careless said. 'You bastard, I smell you, I smell your nervous sweat. Come out and I won't shoot and I swear its the L.M.P. that will handle you and not Zed-Force.'

His breathing was rough and short in the darkness. He had made the mistake of leaving Steele's low-wattage main light on, so that although it didn't penetrate it outlined his big figure in the doorway. And he wasn't lying. In one big hand Careless held a handgun that was obviously an Army-issue Webley.

John knew now that an explanation was impossible. He was an intruder. His hand stole up from where he crouched and felt along the under-rail at the mid-pocket stage of the table. Thank God, there were several balls there. It had been a chance.

He felt very slowly and carefully for the end ball on the rail. He knew now that the slightest click would produce a burst of .455 lead from Careless, who was rattled.

The ball came out silently, cool in his palm. He tensed, raised himself very slowly above the level of the table. His face screwed up. His lips peeled back from his teeth. Then he hurled the small ball at the bulky figure, hearing the thud of it's impact, the grunt of pain that came out of Careless, the clatter of the Webley striking the floor. In the same moment he snatched two more balls out of the rail and stood fully erect, caution thrown to the winds, and flung them across the interval of a few paces, hearing both strike, one with the sickening sound of a melon breaking. Then he paused for a moment, his breath see-sawing in the silent room until there came the heavy crash of Careless's body striking the floor.

John ran out of the room, hurtled down two flights of stairs and dashed out into the night.

Five minutes later he caught a taxi two blocks away directing it to take him to Waterloo Station.

XI

'It was an inside job,' Kyle said to Dawson. 'Fortunately I was first on the scene and turned it into an *outside* job. I came back with Steele and Jenkins at about ten o'clock and all three of us were dying for a drink. Clarke was off duty and Steele rang and rang for Careless until he lost his temper. He asked me to look for the chap upstairs because Careless loves fooling around at the billiard table and it just so happens that the buzzer in the den is out of order at the moment. He sent Jenkins to see if he could find either Gran or Clarke in their quarters.'

He lit a cigarette. It was Saturday morning and the rain still drummed down. Kyle had insisted on a personal report as there was too much to be said over the telephone.

'Of course I found Careless at once when I snapped the light on, flat out on the floor with his gun beside him and three snooker balls that had hit him and rolled to various points. I took Careless's pulse almost on the run and decided that he was going to be all right. In the scheme of things, the way they are beginning to develop, he doesn't matter much anyway although that sounds callous.'

'Coppers have to be callous,' Dawson said. 'Go on.'

Kyle shrugged. 'You know how we develop a sixth sense. Some of us, anyway. I was disturbed. I was positive that someone in the household had attacked Careless because he had been rumbled doing something far removed from common or garden burglary. I remembered very clearly that the front

99

door had been locked and Jenkins who was first out of the car had let us in with his own key. I also knew that from routine checks I made when I first joined them that every room on the ground floor is burglar-proofed except a rather obscure and not easily noticeable one in the pantry.'

'And it was shut?' Dawson was fascinated.

Kyle said impatiently, 'Let me get to that. Steele's bedroom light was on. I shot through there and checked, but there was no sign of disorder or interference. Incidentally that is one hell of a bedroom, I'll tell you about it when there's time. Anyway, at this stage I ran down the stairs and told Steele. Jenkins had just got back from trying to find Clarke and Gran who had both gone out. Naturally they charged upstairs, while I dashed through to the kitchen and found that the pantry window was, as you've suggested, *shut*. I opened it. I took my shoe off, tapped only just hard enough on the outside to break a little glass into my hand. I put the glass down on the floor below the window, leaving the window open. Then I rushed back upstairs, not more than two or three minutes behind the others. Steele with his military background, and Jenkins who is a tough little bastard, were handling things sensibly. Jenkins went down again to call the ambulance and I told Steele about the window.

'Did he seem satisfied?'

'Yes.' Kyle nodded. 'He likes me and to be frank I like him too. He was upset, of course. He and Careless have been together for many years. But he was all common sense too. He even said, "Well, I'm insured to the hilt, I'm just sorry about Tim." Then we snoused around and decided that the "burglar" had been discovered before he could take anything of value. The ambulance boys removed Careless and I telephoned the local nick and two chaps came and did a routine investigation. Needless to say, I showed them the window. They were quite happy to accept my interpretation of events.'

Dawson considered Kyle with fascinated interest. 'Who was it, why did he do it, and why did you cover up for him?'

100

'It was John Willoughby. The little bastard got lost in a limbo yesterday because everyone else was very busy. I've established that he left the Ministry in mid-afternoon when it was already dark. He was due to catch a late train to visit his father. He had about three hours to kill. Kyle spread his hands. 'I suppose he could produce any one of those vague alibis like "I spent my time playing the one-armed bandits or watching a movie", but I know it was him because everyone else was involved and of course you know about the *Time* magazine thing which had got me puzzled and put him under my eye. *Why* he did it is the reason I'm here, and why I covered up for him because if I hadn't opened that window any sound copper would have regarded him as the prime suspect and I do *not* want this chap hauled in on a silly little thing like a charge of assault. There is far more to it than meets the eye, truism though that may be. Willoughby had a purpose and I want to know what it was.'

'What do you think it might have been? Have any ideas?'

Kyle got quite noisy out of sheer frustration. 'I'm *damned* if I know! Maybe Willoughby doesn't know himself. Which brings me to my purpose. I want to do a little burglary of my own.' He told Dawson what he wanted to do.

Dawson sighed. 'Oh well, we get delinquent policemen. If you're had, I will state that you have been behaving quaintly recently.'

Kyle smiled. 'Fair enough. Then when I've served my sentence and come out of Work Force – if I ever do – I'll kill you and emigrate.'

Dawson said, 'Ernie, don't worry, we'll look after you.'

'Thank you kindly,' Kyle said.

Dawson relaxed a little. 'The kid visited his father last night. You know that there has been bad blood between them. How did it turn out?'

'He won't say. Or he doesn't say. He is still alive and so is the Duke of Narsham. I have heard that in the past on Willoughby's rare visits, his father exhibits him like a monkey in a cage and makes him show off his ability as a marksman under floodlights.'

'At *night*?'

'Yes. Shooting under those conditions is very difficult but I believe Willoughby's ability is incredible.'

Dawson said quietly. 'If you are worried about young Willoughby in so far as his relationship with General Steele is concerned, then I don't like the additional fact that he is such an expert shot.'

Kyle got up. He said, 'I can't say that it is his relationship with Steele. He is so temperamental that he might have it in for one of the others. But if it is Steele, then all I can say is that I agree with you, which makes two of us who are worried.' Then he picked up his coat and went out into the cold.

The Willoughby silver glittered on Mary's round oak dining table. Candles made the light low. Clarke, whose services had been offered by Steele as a gesture, was a competent and unobtrusive servitor. Wine shone ruby red in the glasses. Conversation rattled noisily around, bouncing from mouth to mouth.

'Did you shoot it yourself?' Brixton asked Mary, and drew a laugh.

'No, John did.' She looked ravishingly beautiful in a black dress with a deep décolletage. 'I will have you know that this is ibex, smuggled in from Spain, marinated in wine and certain exotic herbs the names of which I will not reveal, larded with fat bacon and finally cooked by my tender hands.'

'It is magnificent.' Brixton said. In fact she had deliberately chosen venison, thinking it suitable for this very masculine meal at which only one woman was present.

There was a chorus of agreement. Hansom asked, 'How's poor Tim? That was a nasty business.'

Steele said, 'He will be all right thanks to the strength of the Careless skull which is constructed on doughty lines.'

'Can he remember what happened?'

'Not a thing. He has pre and post-amnesia which I'm told is fairly common with concussion.'

'And where, pray, are your two bodyguards?' Bingham-Pope asked with mock severity. 'The P.M. will be furious if he hears that you have attended a dinner without your watch-dogs.'

'I told them to go out and bloody well get drunk.' Steele watched moodily while Clarke topped up his glass. 'They hate each other so they will more likely shoot it out in the billiard room.'

There was general laughter. Brixton said, 'Kyle seems a likely sort of fellow. Very competent.'

Steele nodded. He had been in a more serious mood than usual this evening for which, Brixton thought, he could hardly be blamed. 'He is very competent indeed. Far more than I first thought. You should have seen the way he handled that burglary last night. As for Holland, I wish to blazes Campbell would send him back to Canada to be happy in his work.'

All of them knew the hit-man's background. 'Strange chap,' Brixton observed. 'I've seen very little of him, of course, but all he seems to do is sit around and read. And I noticed tonight, Jack, that the fellow seems to have something wrong with his left arm.'

Steele suddenly became more interested. 'That's true, I also saw it. He's hurt it somehow but he isn't telling. Pops pain-killers as though they're going out of fashion.'

Clarke, who had been moving around the table with the wine, said unexpectedly, 'Kyle did it.'

'*What?*' Steele's head jerked up. 'What's that, Nobby?'

'It's a fact,' Clarke said solemnly. 'Holland hired three retired bovver boys to give Kyle the works but the copper cleaned up the lot, came back to the house and tore the muscle in Holland's left shoulder. He even told Holland the symptoms he was going to have the next day. Then Kyle took his gun away from him, emptied it, threw it back at

Holland and walked out of the room whistling "Rock-a-bye-baby". Tim was hanging around in the background and saw it all.'

There was a momentary silence and then a sudden roar of laughter.

'God, that's rich, that's bloody rich!' Steele pounded the table while Clarke walked away grinning. 'And he didn't say a word to any of us!'

'I would like to meet this Kyle of yours,' Mary smiled. 'He sounds fascinating.'

'Send him up to me,' Brixton chuckled, 'to teach my lads unarmed combat. The modern artilleryman is a small bespectacled boffin who does complicated equations in his leisure moments for fun.'

More laughter resounded, especially from Steele, whose mood had now completely changed. John Willoughby, pale and quiet so far, received a hefty slap on the back. 'What's the matter with you, young John, cat got your tongue tonight?'

He had struck just the right moment. By the administration of many heavy whiskies and a lot of wine, John had just then begun to right himself after a whole day of worry and depression over the incident with Careless. Now the bow-string tension that had been eating at him from within like a hag fell away.

'To be quite honest with you, sir,' he said, 'I have a hangover.'

Steele's laugh clattered out. 'The old man laid it on a bit heavily last night, eh? But he's all right? That business between you settled? Hatchet buried and all that?'

'Entirely,' John Willoughby lied.

'Well, then, I suppose you had cause to celebrate. What you need is a hair of the dog. Here, Nobby, bring some bloody wine you horrible little man!'

From the kitchen came a cry of pretended despair. 'I can't pull the flippin' corks fast enough!'

Conversation rose to babble-level. Eyes sparkled. Faces

glowed pinkly in the candlelight reflection of the wine. Mary excused herself briefly saying, 'I must help Clarke with the pudding; the poor man doesn't know his way around.'

Nigel Fox-Carrington had had too much to drink. It showed in his eyes and a little in his manner when he grinned slackly and said, 'I'm deeply hurt by Charles's remark about the absence of your watchdogs. With me around, who needs Kyle and the other feller?' He produced a bibulous belch and added, 'I say, I'm frightfully sorry!'

'In your present condition,' Steele laughed, 'I wouldn't trust you to guard a prostitute's poodle.'

'I'm a damn sight more sober than Phil.' Fox-Carrington winked drunkenly at the artilleryman. 'There he sits imbibing, with all his responsibilities.' He went owl-eyed suddenly as the wine, on top of many whiskies finally caught up with him and he swayed in his chair. 'Frightful responsibilities, eh Phil? Defending England from the bloody Reds. Might be called upon at any time. Midnight. Dawn. The world is in such a sorry state. That red telephone in your office in deeper Northumberland rings and a voice says, "Turn the Guns on Russia", and you know you're about to destroy a million or so people . . .'

'Nigel!' Bingham-Pope's hand went out and touched the Guards officer's arm. 'Nigel you . . .'

'The damn fool is drunk!' Brixton snapped. 'That's classified.'

'Or it says, "Turn the guns on China".' Fox-Carrington swayed again. 'What do you knock out? Peking only? Shanghai? Two million people.' He began to shake with drunken laughter, bringing up his napkin to mop his eyes while all the other men at the table went silent, staring at him. 'My God, who knows when you will be told to "turn the Guns on London," eh, old chap?'

No one said anything for a moment. Then Fox-Carrington turned bloodshot eyes on Steele and mumbled, 'Jesus, Jack, I seem to have got myself frightfully pissed.'

John Willoughby stared at the Guardsman. Steele said, 'You have become somewhat of a lout, sir, Kindly leave the table. I will tender Lady Mary apologies.'

Fox-Carrington heaved himself upright. He lurched, recovered himself, then weaved his way across the lounge to the door where he fumbled for a moment at the latch, got it open, swayed in the doorway, shouted ' 'Night, all!' and was gone with a slither of unsteady footsteps.

They sat silently until his drunken laughter faded away. Bingham-Pope said worriedly, 'When that air hits him he's going to pass out and it's frightfully cold.'

Steele considered for a moment. Then he said grimly, 'When a man I thought to be a gentleman reverts to childhood then he is answerable for the consequences. Let him find his own taxi.'

'I'll go after him.' John jumped to his feet, his cheeks flushed.

'Not if you wish to remain my employ. Sit down, boy.' Steele turned his back on John as Mary came through with a tray laden with glasses of syllabub. 'Zee dessert!' She paused, looked around and frowned. 'What's happened? Where's Nigel?'

Steele began to smile. He said slowly, 'No doubt vomiting his head off in some dirty gutter. He made a pig of himself and as he's a friend of mine I must tender both his and my apologies, Mary. I am very sorry.'

'Don't be silly, it's not your fault, Nigel has always been inclined to overdo things. Now who's for the syllabub?'

Hands stretched forward, talk broke out again. Steele said, 'Look here, let's have some brandy. It's your house. Mary, but not for a woman to do these things. Nobby!'

'He's gone,' Mary said. 'I suspect that he works to the manual. Midnight is midnight. John will get the brandy.' She watched while her brother went to the cabinet, came back with glasses and poured. Her eyes sparkled. 'From the hostess. Your health, gentlemen!'

'No!' Jack Steele said quickly. 'The reverse, my dear. To our hostess!'

They chorused and drank. Steele swigged deeply. His eyes gleamed. 'You're a very sensible woman, my dear. My best wishes.'

She looked at him for a moment. Then: 'Thank you, Jack. Mine too.'

'And now we must be gone.' Steele swigged. 'Gentlemen, we've had a wonderful evening. Let us not overstay our welcome. Let us be gone.'

Extract from a further letter from Mr Ernest Kyle, written as a result of certain queries by the author. Ed.

I reached the helipad first. The chopper was there with the pilot next to it on the hardstand smoking a cigarette. It was cold and there was a strong westerly that chilled me despite my coat. I stayed in the car for about ten minutes and then a Daimler pulled up ahead of me with a roar and Brixton and John Willoughby got out. Both of them were coated and scarved. The good-looking blond Colonel appeared the picture of the professional soldier, pink-cheeked and radiating physical fitness while John seemed to me to have comic-book hangover. But one could never be certain. Sometimes his paleness, the pinched look about his face and his trembly hands were brought about by what ate him from within.

The chopper pilot flicked a salute, got in and started the rotors. I left the car and walked up to the two passengers as they reached the hardstand.

Brixton turned when he saw me. 'Good God, Kyle! Come to see us off at this unearthly hour?'

I smiled. 'Not really, Brixton. I wondered whether you would take me along.'

He studied me for a moment in silence and then grinned. 'Sorry if I sounded condescending, Ernest. I heard a lot about you last night. You are more than welcome. Did Jack okay this jaunt, though?'

I nodded. 'Reluctantly, because it means he's stuck with Holland. But he's agreed.'

'Fine. You will be most interested, I think.'

We started to walk towards the helicopter, having to raise our voices above the gaining engine noise. 'I was amazed to read about Fox-Carrington,' I said. 'What a way to die!'

John Willoughby said, 'Do you not think there is an indication of foul play?'

Brixton turned to answer and found that Willoughby had stopped and we had gone on, so he had to swing about to address the pale young man over a distance of yards.

'What on earth do you mean by that?' he asked sharply.

John Willoughby trembled but he answered stubbornly, 'How many drunks get poured out nightly into London's winter streets? Thousands, I should imagine. And how many die? I've never read of any.'

'On the contrary, I have,' Brixton said crisply. 'Tucked away in the middle of a newspaper, but I've seen this kind of report. Ernest?' His blue eyes flicked towards me.

'It happens all the time,' I said. 'In fact, regularly. It's just that the deaths are not newsworthy unless the dead man was well known or an important figure, which is rarely the case. It's mostly the hobos, the junkies, the alcoholics who're killed by cold.'

Brixton shrugged. 'There you are. Policemen and soldiers get used to death, young John; you must not be so upset and start reading all sorts of sinister meanings into the manner of his death just because you knew him and liked him. Nigel had the misfortune to pass out behind a hedge and nobody saw him.' He looked about at the bleak skies. 'In this weather he didn't stand a chance. Now come on, lad, let's go.'

We conversed very little during the ride to Brixton's headquarters. The chopper was freezing and draughty. Willoughby and I sat behind the pilot and Brixton. My teeth chattered. Willoughby got even paler. I was becoming convinced that the tip of my nose was frostbitten when Brixton turned and shouted. 'Scottish Border not far ahead. We're going down!'

It had been snowing at the Base. I got out and jumped down on to hard-packed snow and the others piled out behind me as a young Major pelted towards us from a line of Nissen-type prefabs and skidded to a stop, peeling off a salute as Brixton emerged. What little I had got out of Willoughby on the way up had been Brixton's wisecrack about his small, boffin-like, equation-loving artillerymen. This one might have been a boffin but he was also about five feet seven inches of hard-packed muscle.

'Colonel! And this would be Lord John Willoughby. Welcome, Lord John.' His hard eyes regarded me with indecision coupled with mild distaste.

'Kyle,' I said. 'Detective Inspector, Special Branch, assigned to Mr Steele's household by the Assistant Commissioner on the instructions of the Prime Minister.'

The military are endeared to this kind of introduction. He didn't even catch the barb on the end of my tongue. Instead his manner changed entirely while Brixton said, 'This is Major Douglas Barraclough, my Adjutant. Otherwise, Doug, you guessed correctly, so the introductions have been performed. Let's get warm.'

We trotted across the snow and I suspected that this was part of a regimen instituted by Brixton to keep his men fit, because it was enough of a distance for a vehicle to have been used. Life was hard and Brixton was making it harder. Bored, lazy men are less efficient and more difficult to control.

Brixton explained as he ran, without once pausing to puff, that the Nissens housed the men of the Regiment, the N.C.O.s, two Messes, and the ablution block. Rounding this complex we came upon what one might call the modern version of Officer's Row – neat little prefabs, each separated by sere winter hedges in deference to the British love of privacy. Through the snow, which had been a light fall, I could see the tiny front gardens and neatly gravelled walks. The houses were gingham-curtained as though to defy winter's severe hand and I suspected that summer would present a very different picture.

We hauled up at the first of these prefabs, no more or less pretentious than its neighbours, and Brixton marched ahead with a brisk, 'Enter my humble domicile,' not even giving us a chance to blow so I had to puff rather noisily inside the small lounge.

'Sarah must be around unless she's next door.' Brixton offered cigarettes and lit them. 'I think we'll have a cup of tea first, Douglas, and then take these chaps down to the sites. Then we can adjourn to the Mess for drinks and lunch. Have you got the forms?'

'Yes indeed.' Barraclough unbuttoned a tunic pocket and produced an envelope from which he extracted two printed forms in which we undertook to keep secret so much that, after perusing the old-fashioned legal phraseology, I had the feeling I would be obliged on pain of severe penalty, to refuse to name the types of weed growing at the Base. Willoughby and I had both to sign and swear, 'So help me God' before Brixton who added his own name as C.O.

We had just completed the task when Brixton's wife joined us. She had been for a walk, and was towing a perambulator from which emanated coos and gurgles which appeared constantly to delight her. Clad in what amounted to nothing more than ski garb, she still looked like a beautiful woman and apparently unaware of it, which made her, as I recorded in my diary,

even more delightful. She is a lady to her fingertips and I suspect that she comes from one of England's foremost families. She was certainly not at all overawed by having a lord in her lounge drinking tea and eating anchovy sandwiches.

Surprisingly, I've always been rather good with babies, even though all I seem to be able to produce as I bend over cot or pram is a fatuous, piping 'Cuckoo, cuckoo!' And this mite, with glowing pink cheeks, produced a gummy beam and because I had done my bit successfully everyone laughed and applauded.

As the Base was a permanent establishment, the married officers normally ate in their homes. Bachelors used the Mess for their meals and all the officers drank there, but everyone came together on special occasions or when V.I.P.s turned up. I didn't fall into that second category but Lord John Willoughby did.

Just as we finished with tea, a vehicle pulled up and we went out into the cold again, travelling a comparatively short distance to a cluster of low structures that resembled block-houses. Brixton told the driver to wait, produced keys and took us into a brightly-lit, concrete-floored space with a bank of elevators. On our right was a door through which I could see tiers of panels containing the most incredibly complicated-looking gauges, dials and switches.

'This is N-Troop, Y-Battery,' Brixton said as the lift doors jumped open and we whined downwards. 'What you're going to see are Drumhead Intercontinental Ballistic Missiles. They are kept in what we call 'silos', in 'hard' launching sites which simply means that they are underground and impervious to attack. Relatively, anyway. You will also see the few Drum-head 2 missiles we have here, which are smaller and have a shorter range and are intended for battlefield support. Military thinking at the moment is that there is little likelihood of a conventional war being fought on England's fair fields, so we are concerned more with the I.C.B.M.s. The DH1 – that of course is short for Drumhead – carries a nuclear warhead only but the DH 2, or Little Brother as it is also known, can be fitted either with a nuclear or conventional-explosive war-head. Even in the latter event it still carries one hell of a punch.'

The doors sprang open again and a speedwalk conveyed us silently for some distance along a brightly-lit tunnel ending with a door that hissed open even as Brixton approached it.

We walked slowly into the vast, brilliantly-lit 'silo' where the giant rocket crouched. It had such an air of menace that I felt my skin crawl, and Willoughby seemed paler than usual.

Barraclough crossed to a panel. He pressed a switch and immediately lights and gauges glowed and flickered. He said quietly,'Way back, we missile-men had a problem in that we used cryogenic propellants, such as liquid oxygen, which meant that the weapon could only be fuelled immediately prior to launching. This, in turn, meant that there had by necessity to be delay in firing, an alarming situation if your firing was defensive, or in retaliation. The problem was solved by the use of noncryogenic propellants which can withstand storage without deterioration.'

'In other words,' John Willoughby said, 'this missile can be fired *now*.'

'Precisely. I'll show you.' He led us back to the speedwalk and we went back up to the room I had seen on my arrival. 'This is the control room. You will notice that the control panel up here has come alive because I switched on below. It works both ways.'

'That can only mean, 'I slowly, beginning to feel clammy, 'that if it were a last minute thing—'

'If it were a desperate situation,' Barraclough nodded, 'and this control room had for example been knocked out, your man down below would do the firing.' He paused and then added, 'He would never know what hit him. The chaps all accept this. When we are on standby, which is most of the time, there is always a man below.'

There was a thoughtful silence. Then Brixton switched off the control panel and we were taken to lunch,

which was first class. We met the rest of the officers who seemed a fine bunch of fellows and were obviously handpicked. Brixton is an exceptional Commanding Officer and his men appear devoted to him. Young Willoughby's mood changed completely. He was flushed, excited, drank a bit much but then it never seems to have any particular effect, and Brixton has obviously taken a liking to him. So much so, that I heard Brixton invite him to the annual Regimental Dinner which takes place on Thursday night. This is a signal honour because by tradition only two guests are allowed. Jack Steele is to be the other, which seems logical when one considers that he and Brixton are best friends, although there is a little doubt about his being able to come. If he can they will bring him up by helicopter jet.

We were due to return to London immediately after lunch, so after a round of handshakes we left immediately for the helicopter pad with Brixton and Barraclough, but we'd hardly got out the door when I patted my packets and said: 'Dammit, Colonel, I've left my cigarettes in your lounge, shan't be a sec.,' and dashed off before he could argue.

Mrs Brixton answered the door with a safety-pin in her mouth, laughing when she realized how she looked. I explained my purpose, collected my packet of cigarettes; I paused over the baby, now sleeping peacefully with its arms upwards on the pillow next to its head in an attitude of surrender.

'She's beautiful.' I straightened. 'Looks just like you.'

She had been smiling as I headed for the door but when her voice stopped me on the threshold and I turned, her expression had become serious.

'Mr Kyle, you are a police officer I believe.'

'Detective Inspector, L.M.P.,' I confirmed.

'You're a very clever man, Mr Kyle, I can tell. You're not going to do anything, are you?' She said, and hesitated.

'No, nothing other than pat myself on the back.' I shrugged and put out my hand. 'The feeling is mutual – you are an extremely clever woman. Goodbye, Mrs Brixton, it has been a pleasure meeting you.'

Then I turned my back and trotted off along the walk.

XII

While Kyle and John flew towards the wilds of Northumberland, Dawson worriedly regarded two Special Branch D.I.s by the names of Carter and North.

'If I had my way I would apprehend the man now.' A feeble sun had broken through but it was still very cold and he stood before the electric fire rubbing his hands together. 'But we have standing orders that in circumstances such as these General Steele wishes the matter to be given as much airing as possible. This is not just a desire for publicity on his part but a sincere belief that a public arrest – or even the shooting of the would-be assassin, the way it was outside Parliament – acts as a deterrent to others of the same mind.'

'There are two schools of thought about that,' Carter said.

'Yes, I know. The Steele School, and ours which is that this kind of thing can have the reverse effect by attracting nut-cases of varying degrees who want a weird kind of limelight, rather on the lines of what happened to the Kennedy family in America years ago.'

'So what do we do?' North asked.

'I have my orders. Let it go ahead. Everything sounds perfectly safe but I always get the willies. I want ten armed men hanging around in different guises just in case. It's at eleven, so you'd better get moving.'

At eleven o'clock precisely Steele stood in his hall with Carter and North. Holland loomed sullenly in the background.

He was never told anything but he sensed that something unusual was going on.

Steele said, 'All right, gentlemen, let's go,' and they walked briskly to the door where a tense Clarke opened it as they arrived, so that they walked outside into the sharp cold without delay.

At the same moment Mr Benjamin Pickles, secreted below the window level of a dilapidated car parked across the street, emerged like Phoenix from the ashes and poked the twin muzzles of his old shotgun out of the window. He pulled back both hammers until they stopped on full cock, sighted down between the barrels at Steele's middle, closed his eyes and pulled both triggers.

He was rewarded by the twin clicks of two firing pins striking dud percussion caps.

The tense group on the steps of Steele's house saw the expression of devastated bewilderment that crossed Mr Pickles's face as he stared in accusation at the seditious shotgun. North and Carter began to run directly towards him while others dashed in from different directions. Only Steele, ordered by some instinct to glance backward at his Zed-Force bodyguard, saw Holland's lips turning down as his Magnum cleared leather and popped into view above the level of his left lapel.

It was too late to stop the shot. But the perfectly aimed bullet, which would have made a hole in the car door about three inches below the window and then in Mr Pickles as well, boomed skyward as Steele's arm swept the weapon upwards.

The Canadian's eyes went yellow with vicious frustration but in almost the same moment Steele's fist connected directly with the point of his jaw and the lights went out for a moment. They came on again when he was lying on the sidewalk with Steele's furious face above him.

'You murdering son of a bitch! You stinking bastard! You saw those cartridges fail!' A polished shoe took Holland in the ribs so hard that he gasped. Steele, with a wild look in his eyes, shouted, 'Get that bastard out of my sight!'

One lone and chilly photographer, who had been hanging around in the hope of the same kind of mischance that had dogged the accident-prone President Ford of America during his term of office, earned himself a small fortune by triggering off his camera to capture a furious Minister of Labour ordering his prone bodyguard back inside the house.

Steele himself straightened as Clarke and a Special Branch man carried the limp Holland indoors. He visibly took hold of himself, stared out at the gathering crowd, then said crisply, 'Right, gentlemen, let's be on our way.'

North and Carter watched him go while they stood on either side of a submissive Mr Pickles. 'That', North said with awe, 'was worth about ten thousand votes.'

XIII

'I can't wait to hear about your trip to Northumberland,'
Dawson said to Ernest Kyle. 'I thought the place was in-
habited by Picts. But trivia first.' He flipped open a file and
donned gold-rimmed glasses. 'Lord John Willoughby's political past at university.' He began to read:

First year, politically inactive. Second year, joined a club
called the 'True Democrats' which was dedicated to the
preservation of Government by the People through Parliament. Was a regular attender of the weekly meetings and
after three months emerged from his shell and began par-
ticipating in the debates and discussions which were
concerned largely with the menaces of Communism and
Fascism. The membership of the club was composed largely
of young men from highly conservative families and several
were titled. Discussion groups also examined Parliamentary
Procedure and Whitehall's place in the running of the
affairs of the country. Of the six ex-members interviewed
at length, all recollected clearly that subject was their most
extreme member if such a word could be used for such an
association. Subject wished to take Democracy to such
lengths as to make it absurd. When overruled or outvoted
he would become extremely heated and shout furiously or
storm out. Rumpuses became so frequent, and subject's
attitude so impossible, that in the end by unanimous vote
he was asked to resign. He did, but created such a furore

that interest waned and within six months the club had ceased to exist. Subject took no further interest in politics and left university not long afterwards.

'That doesn't mean much,' Kyle said sourly. 'Bunch of upper-class lunatic centre.'

Dawson laughed. 'That's as good a way of putting it as any. Did you hear about our friend Mr Pickles?'

'Yes, North told me on my way in. I wonder if the old fool realizes that the Special Branch saved his life? Firing Magnums out of a shotgun with Damascus twist-steel barrels is a rather messy way of committing suicide. I also hope that Little Lord Fauntleroy, who made such a fuss about our bugging Pickles's house, feels a thorough ass.' He reflected for a moment. 'Holland will never forgive Steele. He doesn't stick his neck out unless he is paid a great deal of money but I still wonder whether he will let it pass.'

'Campbell is contemplating pulling him out. You can't push Campbell, so in the meantime the whole household has Holland under their eye. If one considers that this includes tough customers like Clarke, Careless – he'll be back on duty tomorrow – and Jenkins, I wouldn't worry too much, Ernest.'

'I've got enough worries as it is.' Kyle stood up and turned towards the door.

'Hang on, you haven't told me about your Northumberland escapade!'

'I found an interesting baby,' Kyle said, and walked out leaving Dawson staring at the door.

Mr Percy Swindell was seeing his Minister of Labour informally at No. 10. He was a creaky old man with a marked stoop and a switchblade brain. In his young days when the blade was out it had been able to cut like a razor, but when it was in he behaved like the innocuous and bemused turtle he strongly resembled.

Swindell was also a brooder, as his embittered wife could

testify, and ever since his appointment he had been brooding over the fact that the King had made a point of dispensing with the kissing of hands ceremony. Very often he would lie in bed in the mornings and wonder just how he had got into all this, and complained in his squeaky voice to his wife, who would say not one word but reach for the tranquillizers.

He was nevertheless a man whose entire life had been spent in politics and he knew his onions even if he did not tend them very well. A surprising thing was that the Russians were afraid of him. He could bare his tobacco-stained teeth in a snarl as wolverine as any of their statesmen, and both swear and drink them under the table, something he had proved on numerous occasions when he had been Foreign Minister in an earlier Tory government.

The sad fact was that the spring of the switchblade was spent so that the knife seldom emerged and when it did it was blunt. Percy Swindell was verging on senility, and only the turtle remained.

'Have a sherry,' he squeaked to Jack Steele. 'It is genuine Tio Pepe and I have difficulty in getting it. I, the Prime Minister. Strange situation, isn't it?'

Steele signalled his acknowledgement and took a glass. 'It's not really so strange, Prime Minister. We simply cannot pay for what we want to buy. The economic situation is elementary.'

'Well, then I never went to school!' The blade shot out but immediately retreated.

Steele shook his head. 'Prime Minister, I am quite sure we did not meet here to discuss the difficulties of obtaining Tio Pepe. You asked me to come because the General Workers Union have decided to strike if the pay demands they issued today are not met by Wednesday.'

Swindell harrumphed and then said, 'Well, yes, that's true, Steele. Mullins is impossible. I can't stand him. Perhaps the fact that he is an avowed Communist influences me, or the fact that his General Workers Union are asking the impossible. I think he knows it. I think his instructions from Moscow are to bring the nation to its knees.'

Steele said almost idly, 'No doubt.' Then, 'We were non-swimmers wearing water-wings and keeping our heads above the surface even if the air was leaking out. Now our water-wings have been slashed and we must surely drown very quickly.'

Swindell's bottom lip began to tremble. 'My God, Steele, England does not want this terrible illness. Take it, my boy, take it please and cure it quickly.'

Steele seemed to ponder. Then the rugged figure stirred. 'I will brook no interference, Prime Minister. I must make that clear. I must be allowed to handle this in my way or I do not handle it at all.'

'I give you *carte blanche*,' said Swindell. Two senile tears brimmed in his eyes. They lipped his eyelids and slid slowly down his cheeks. 'My God, my boy, I do believe England is dying.'

Stake-out men had been in position outside Mary's flat that morning from an hour before Kyle had spoken to Dawson. They had unfortunately chosen a day on which she had no photographic appointments and so they grew cold and irritable while she slept late, made herself a salad for lunch, and spent the afternoon with household chores. She was an industrious young woman who enjoyed the culinary arts and thus, although a cleaning woman came four times a week, she had no permanent maid.

At four o'clock, while she made herself a cup of tea, Steele and Bingham-Pope were jetting to Birmingham to meet Joe Mullins, leader of the General Workers Union, with the object of hammering out a place and time at which they would conduct negotiations the following day. They knew that they were coming up against the strongest man they had yet encountered, and spoke deeply and earnestly while they flew.

Also at four o'clock, in Birmingham, Joe Mullins was making love to his mistress, a girl by the name of Irma Saler. He kept his own hours, and the affair had been conducted under a cloak of great secrecy because Mullins not only loved his thin, tight-lipped wife in his own fashion but he had married late and had a six-year-old angel-faced son who was the apple of his eye. He knew that if his wife were to discover this illicit union she would immediately divorce him. She was a religious person of high principle but there was no doubt in his mind that she would not only do this, but obtain custody of Mullins Junior as well. Apart from the unsavoury aspect of adultery, she knew enough about some of his dealings to convince any Court that he would not be a fit custodian parent. So Joe Mullins met his lover at different rooms, apartments, and motels, and would not move an inch before the head of the squad of muscle men he kept hanging around his headquarters could assure him that the place was 'clean'.

Only at seven o'clock did Mary leave her flat. She was fashionably dressed and took a taxi to an address approximately three miles away.

At ten minutes past seven the telephone rang in Steele's house in Belgravia. Clarke took the call, which was from a young woman who asked whether this was the number at which she could contact Ernest Kyle. The Special Branch man happened to pass by at that moment and Clarke signalled him. Kyle spoke to a girl whom he addressed as Nancy, and regretfully turned down an invitation to a party on Friday night. Ten minutes later he left the house, telling Clarke that he would be out for some time. He knew that John had enough work to keep him busy for another three hours.

As Kyle hailed a taxi, the stake-out men were removed from the vicinity of Lady Mary Willoughby's apartment. From now on, Kyle was on his own.

The taxi dropped him off a block away from the flat and

Kyle walked briskly along in the chill evening air, entered the building and took the stairs because he already knew that Mary's flat was on the first floor and that there was no concierge, only a spinster caretaker who occupied one of the ground floor flats and, unusually, did not pry.

The first floor passage was ill-lit by one bulb in the ceiling and was deserted. His steps rang upon the floor until he stopped at Mary's door. Moving quickly now, he produced from his coat a strange device which resembled a pistol except that the 'barrel' was flat and almost as thin as a needle. Making no sound at all, he gently inserted it into the keyhole, fiddled a moment, and then allowed the door to swing open. He withdrew his pick, entered quickly and shut the door silently. The whole operation had taken less than a minute.

He removed his coat and made a quick inspection of the entire dwelling, moving from room to room with the silence and speed of a cat. It took him no more than another five minutes to locate and familiarize himself with the living area, the kitchen, bathroom and toilet, Mary's room and the spare room used by John. He came back deliberately to the lounge, checked the lay-out in his mind, then went quickly to John's room where he shut the door and switched on the low-wattage bedside light.

The room was plainly furnished. There was a bed, a built-in clothes closet, a bookshelf, a chest of drawers and a small bedside table with a single drawer. Kyle headed instinctively and automatically for it. It was locked, and he had to use his pick again. But when he got the drawer open it contained only some loose coins, a few letters and bills, and a spare watch.

'Damn!' Kyle said quietly. What he was looking for was the record of day-to-day events kept by a man who was, to use his own words, a 'compulsive diarist'. Kyle himself kept a diary and he was laying everything on the belief that when a man records his life, day in and day out, he is doing so privately in a world of his own and will neither conceal nor repress anything, including murder.*

He looked around. The main thing to bear in mind was that the room was essentially a *spare* room, used by John in the past only when he had come to London. Even now his occupancy could be regarded only as semi-permanent because it depended upon the strength of his sister's charity. Wherever the diary was kept or hidden, the place had to be as tenuous as the stay of its owner.

Kyle went back to the bookshelf, examining the spines of the books there. They were all reasonably new and probably the property of Mary except one, which was a reprint of one of G. A. Henty's memorable books for boys. Kyle pulled it out and found himself holding only the shell of a book, two hard covers and the spine, while in the same moment John Willoughby's diary fell with a small slap on to the carpet. It had been brilliantly hidden by the inherently suspicious young man and only Kyle's years of training, and the determination to get to a goal, by endlessly repetitive work if necessary, had found it. No matter how beset John had found himself by enemies real or imaginary, he was supremely confident of the pristine safety of the diary and could write and write and write no matter the circumstances. Kyle was reminded of the Crusader who locks his wife in a chastity belt, throws the key into a stream and goes on his way. Just as the hardy warrior might do battle in the contentment of the knowledge that his wife was inviolable, so had John written in the unshakeable belief that his scribblings were secure.

'What an incredibly clever chap!' Kyle murmured in genuine admiration. He picked it up, very pleased with himself. The only question now was just how honest John Willoughby was with himself.

Kyle flipped the pages. Then he started at the most recent

*See for example the diaries of Sir William Dugdale and Bullstrode Whitelocke, whose authors had no idea that they would ever see the light of day and are full of indiscretions.

entry and worked backwards. Sunday contained a short account of the visit to the Missile Base,

> into which Kyle intruded most rudely. If I had been Brixton I would have told him to go to blazes. He is a snooping obnoxious fellow. [Kyle chuckled and read on.] Brixton is a most charming person, and I consider it a great honour to have been invited to the Regimental Dinner. The only aspect that sticks in my craw is his friendship with Jack Steele. As I have said before, it is with regret that I have had completely to revise my opinion of our Minister of Labour. And I feel a confounded idiot for disregarding Mary's well-meant warning. She was right. Since the discovery of the uniform and the death of Nigel Fox-Carrington a conclusion has begun to formulate in my mind which I am not prepared even to put on paper until I have more facts. I am a very worried man.

Kyle frowned. Uniform? What the hell was he talking about? And here he was going on about Fox-Carrington's death the way he had at the helicopter.

He went on and read the entry of a most conscientious and thorough diarist:

> I am afraid that I was obliged to leave Friday and Saturday blank until now. I returned from my visit to Father exhausted and heavy with liquor, yet still so tense that I had to take 20mg before sleep claimed me. Saturday after the late dinner, was as bad. So I am writing this section at six on Sunday morning with my eye on the clock because I have not all that much time before Brixton and I head for the helipad. I think, though, that I have the time to record the events of Friday and Saturday and I hope that today will not run on so long that I am too tired to record my visit to the base. *Friday:* I had determined, as I have already recorded, to do some snooping without really

knowing what I was after. It was a miserable day with rain pouring down – London at it's gloomiest. Due to the administrative lacks of Steele and/or Hansom and Jenkins, I was left in a sort of vortex at the Ministry and made my decision around mid-afternoon to investigate Steele's house.

Kyle read on while John Willoughby described his adventures on the second floor. Totally absorbed, he said only, in great puzzlement, 'Field Marshal? What the hell . . .' and then 'Yes, it had to be the little bastard, I thought I was right,' when he read of the attack upon Careless, which concluded with,

I don't know how the taxi driver didn't spot my distress. My breath was see-sawing in and out of my lungs and I was convinced that I was going to pass out at any moment. Fortunately I have experienced these manifestations of excessive nervous tension before – I experience wave after wave of weakness flowing through my body and it is a most alarming thing – so I took 15mg before boarding the train and fortunately found myself with a saloon car so that by the time Swanby met me at the station I had had two hefty whiskies. These, combined with the Valium, did no more than reduce me to normal.

Father still resembles a modern-day Falstaff, lecherous, veiny, flint-eyed and evil. When I saw the floodlights I knew that he was going to use me as his performing monkey again but this did not bother me particularly. I know my capabilities with guns and a little showing off gratifies the ego. But he did not come out to meet me, which I rather did expect. Our visits have been reduced only to formal family occasions such as Christmas and Mary's birthday, so that we had not seen each other for a long time. In the drawing-room there was an assemblage of about fourteen guests of the strangest appearance and a complete conglomerate of ages and walks of life. He said in front of them, 'Well, John my boy! So nice to see you agin! These are my fwends. Hope you've got all that silly nonsense out of your head about your dear Mother, eh?'

I had to struggle desperately not to strike him, but I had promised myself on the way out that I would allow him one chance, apart from which the incident with Careless was still very much in the forefront of my mind. So I just nodded, while the guests tittered and I realized that he had been filling them in on my background before I arrived. I ground my teeth and got stuck into the whisky the way everyone else was doing and after about half an hour Father slapped me on the back and said, 'Ah you weady, John my boy?' while he cuddled his latest whore, an angelic-faced blonde who models for the raincoat trade. The thought of that beautiful face and body being straddled by that old satyr is positively nauseating.

We traipsed out to the Skeet range and I shot ping-pong balls off a water spout, lit six matches by grazing the heads with .22 bullets, and ended up my act by sending an empty jam tin flying into the air with my first shot from the Kit Gun that Mary likes, keeping it flying around with the impact of each successive bullet.

When we got back to the house the drinking started again while we were served spit-roast sucking pig and one of the better wines from the Hacienda. Things developed into a sort of Bachanalian orgy and Father's angelic whore stripped completely naked and lay on the table while wine was poured over her. The males in the group were starting to pull off their pants when I walked out and found Frame on the steps. He was white-faced and shaking.

'Come on, sir,' he said. 'Forget about trains, I'll drive you back to London, I've nothing to do.'

I thanked him and he brought the Rolls around and we pulled away. Neither of us spoke for at least half the journey until I said, 'Frame, it's got much worse.'

He nodded, staring ahead. 'In the beginning, when you were a youngster, he was just a roaring old bastard, with him and your Mother running their separate affairs. Nothing really unique. Now it's like what you saw tonight. I think the booze has turned him mad.'

'I don't know what to do,' I said.

He slowed down and grabbed my arm with fingers like steel. 'Don't go back, sir. It's very bad for you. I'm pulling out myself after twenty years. Me, the Missus, and three big kids. We're all in agreement.'

I stared at him in astonishment. 'Frame! But where will you go?'

'Spain,' he said. 'This country's 'ad it, anyway. I liked being an Englishman. I was proud of being an Englishman. But all that's gone now. As you know I can handle the lingo after all those years of going across, and so can the rest of the family. Miguel has landed me a plumb job on the estate of a cousin of King Carlos. I've got a written contract to prove it.'

I stared at the highway slipping between our wheels. In odd places the weeds had broken through the asphalt. Every few miles we would pass an old wrecked car, stripped of its usable parts but rusty and abandoned.

'Frame. All I can say is good luck.'

Neither of us said another word until he pulled up outside Mary's flat. Frame seemed deeply emotional. 'Goodbye, sir. I hope we might meet across there.'

I shook my head. 'I don't think so. I am *of* this country. I don't know if you understand what I mean.'

'Yes, I do.' He hesitated and then blurted out, 'John – I used to call you that when you were a lad – I know that you have worked out your own theory as to the manner in which your Mother died. It got you cut off.' He stopped abruptly.

I began to shake. 'Frame, what do you mean? What are you getting at?'

'Just this.' His eyes glittered at me. 'It's true. I can say no more.'

I stood in the street watching the big car roar away until its tail lights were like twin fireflies, and then gone.

Kyle stared at the entry a long time. Then he whispered 'Poor little twisted bastard,' and went on to the account of Saturday's events which were concerned almost entirely with the dinner party at Mary's flat. While he read, Steele and Bingham-Pope were being shown into Joe Mullins's headquarters where the obese, gross-featured Union Czar sat behind an imposing desk. The office was panelled, tastefully furnished, and warm.

Before they could be seated, Mullins's flat North Country accents rang out. 'Gentlemen, I want to make myself plain. I am prepared to laugh with you over a drink. There is a completely stocked bar behind my back.' He stabbed a button and a section of the panelling slid back to prove his point. He hit it again and it shut. 'But I want to make it clear that I do not intend to negotiate with you in any manner whatsoever, for whatever purpose, and if that is the reason why you are here, which I presume it must be, I do not intend to rise, I do not intend to shake your hands, and I do not intend to offer you a chair. All I want is for you to meet my Union's demands by midday tomorrow or *get out!*' His fist crashed down on the desk and his eyes flamed. He ground out: 'Are you blind, Steele? My God, man, don't you realize that I command four million workers? Can't you see when you're beaten?'

They knew that the office was bugged. Steele said icily, that little curved smile appearing at the corner of his mouth, 'We will meet tomorrow morning in the middle of the cricket pitch at a village called Little Sephton. Only you and I will be present. We will be wearing only shirt and trousers, no matter the weather. Your muscle men and Mr Bingham-Pope here may occupy the tiny cricket pavilion which is the only structure within eyesight, so that there will be no possibility of the use of ultra-sensitive electronic devices by either side. There, you and I will discuss a settlement of your Union's pay demands.'

Mullins's face had gone a dull red. He curved his big hands as though he wanted to claw at Steele like a grizzly bear. He heaved himself upright, his bulk quivering. 'My God how dare you talk to me like that! How dare you dictate terms as though I was a bloody lackey, didn't you hear what I said? Are you deaf? By God I . . .'

He was interrupted by a tap on the door and a senior clerk entered bearing a small packet. He appeared terrified. 'Joe, this has been sent by Special Delivery marked "very urgent, private and confidential attention Mr Mullins only" and it's been put through the machine, so its clean. He dropped it on Mullins's desk and scurried out.

'Shit!' Mullins tore at it, ripping off the brown paper and string. But while he did it he talked. 'Steele, I've a mind to deal with you, the way you talk. I know how you handled the Dockworkers. I know how you handled the Railwaymen too. You've laid down the bloody law for so long you think you can do it to anyone. Well I'm going to tell you something. You've come across a very hard nut you can't crack.' With quivering fingers he produced a small box out of the mess of paper. It had the name of a leading photographic dealer printed all over it and Mullins went quiet. All he had to do was lift the top flap and look inside. After a strained, reluctant pause, he did.

There was a long silence while all the blood drained out of his face. He stared for seconds at the top photograph and then, as though driven mad, snatched out the rest and thumbed through them while his face

went completely chalky and I genuinely thought that we were going to have a coronary on our hands. I have never seen a man so completely shattered. It must have been a minute before his legs gave way and he sprawled back into his huge executive-type chair, his lips going slack. He stared at us with the eyes of a dying deer while we remained on our feet saying nothing and giving no visible reaction. In this terrible silence he finally lifted a shaky hand to that bar-button of his, heaved his tremendous bulk upward, and went to the bar where he poured a huge gin and drank it neat, using both hands to steady the glass. He poured and drank yet another while the same silence ran on and when he was half-way through it – he had his back to us so that all we could see was his enormous backside encased in outsize trousers – he turned his head sideways, not looking at us, and said 'You filthy bastards. I'll 'ave you know I've done a thing or two in my time but never . . . this'. He let his voice trail away for a long time and then in an empty tone dropped some words into the silence. 'What time did you say?'

Jack Steele said, 'Eleven thirty,' and we turned about and left the room.*

Back in London in the silence of Mary's flat, Kyle read the concluding remarks John had made about the dinner party: *What he said, the attempts that were made to stop him, and the fact that Clarke left at almost exactly the same time, I can only regard as highly significant.*

Kyle shook his head. No. Willoughby was on the wrong track. He seemed to want to be. Bingham-Pope had touched Fox-Carrington's sleeve to shut him up. After what Kyle had seen at the Rocket Base it was obvious that the older man had been afraid that Fox-Carrington was going to come out with classified information. Brixton had made a similar but more aroused – even angry – indication.

And what had the Guardsman said? Kyle examined the words carefully. In his drunken state he had suggested that Brixton might at some time or other be called upon to let

*See *Gird me with Steele* by Charles Bingham-Pope, page 246 *et seq.*

130

loose his missiles of war at Communist cities. He was under the impression that he was being funny. It was asinine but not remarkable. It would seem that it had to be Fox-Carrington's final remark, 'My God, who knows when you will be told to turn the guns on London, eh, old chap?' that had had such an impact on John Willoughby, and then only because this time Fox-Carrington had been referring to his own country.

What had Fox-Carrington intended? Had it not been a clumsy and jocular exaggeration that London was in such a mess that Brixton might have to drop a missile on it?

Finally, there was the coincidence of Clarke taking his leave at the same time, or very nearly the same time, as the Guardsman. Was John inferring that Clarke had been responsible for the death of his employer's friend?

'No,' Kyle said out loud. He paged back to Friday, the day of John's interview with Steele, and read on quickly, glancing at his watch, pausing only at Thursday where John briefly described his childhood. At that stage he said only, 'Incredible'. Then he returned to Friday and put the diary flat on the bedside table under the lamp. From his pocket he produced a small and flat camera, put the viewfinder to his eye, held the camera about a foot above the diary, and pressed the exposure button. Turning the pages with his left hand, he photographed each page until the end, so that for a minute there was no sound except the continuous tiny clicking of the camera. Then Kyle heaved a sigh, returned it to his pocket, closed the diary and put it back exactly where he had found it.

From John's room he returned to the lounge and went to the telephone where he dialled rapidly. When a voice answered sharply at the other end he said, 'I'm calling from a friend's place. That sneaky feeling of mine turned out to be right. I'd like to see Uncle tomorrow, and I don't care if you have to bring him back from Iceland or wherever the hell he is.'

'He's just 'phoned. Your appointment is for ten thirty tomorrow morning and I'm coming with you.'

'All right. And I want some film processed in a hurry. I'll drop it at Nancy's place.'

'You will have it by nine tomorrow.' There was a pause. 'Are things that bad?'

'It's for Uncle to say. But they could be.' Then he replaced the receiver put on his coat and left the flat, allowing the latch to click gently behind him.

He had reached the street and walked no more than ten paces when he saw a young woman alighting from a cab. She had her back to him and his attention had been caught more by the arresting roundness of her small bottom when her face came around in profile and he recognised her instantly. It was Mary Willoughby and he agreed with himself, while his stomach slid briefly down to his feet and bounced back again, that he had cut things very fine indeed.

She hurried into the apartment building looking neither left nor right and Kyle went on, but from briskness his pace dwindled to a dawdle and he finally stopped in front of an unlit shop window from where he looked back, taking his time over the lighting of a cigarette.

An idea had come to him and the more he thought about it the more appealing it seemed. He did not want to rush into things, so he sauntered across the road to an Indian restaurant where he had a *Khurma* that seemed to consist more of rice than anything else and washed it down with half a bottle of acidulous win. His waiter was also the proprietor, and when his bill was brought Kyle said, 'That was worth half of what you're asking. Here's the half and don't threaten to call a policeman because I am one. Having difficulty getting meat?'

The Indian gazed ruefully at the notes Kyle tendered. He seemed to want to argue the toss but then changed his mind and said with a shrug, 'If things don't improve I close in about two weeks. I've been here for twenty-five years. The jet-set used to eat at this place.'

Kyle had now made up his mind. He walked back to the apartment building, used the same stairs, and knocked on the same door.

Mary answered, looking puzzled when she saw the strange face. Then her expression changed and she said firmly, 'I'm sorry, I don't need encyclopedias, brushes, face creams or whatever else you're selling. Good night.'

He put his foot in the door. All he said was 'Kyle.'

'Well.' She looked down at his foot. 'Is there any need to play the heavy?'

'I wanted to keep the door open,' he said mildly.

'Come in and sit down. Have a drink, too. Whisky?'

He chose John's favourite, the rocking chair. 'Thank you.'

From the cabinet she said, 'You didn't come to visit John. You know that he's tied up.'

'Yes.' He lit a cigarette.

'Are you checking me out?'

'No.'

'Then what brings you here?'

'Curiosity.'

'In what respect?'

'I wanted to see how a lady reacted to a common copper.'

She came back with drinks of Willoughby calibre. 'How am I shaping?'

'Rudely. I don't like being cross-examined. Cheers.'

'Cheers. Rudeness is a reaction to sullenness.'

'We seem to have got off on the wrong foot.'

'Indeed. We've known each other for about four minutes but the dialogue sounds like four years. Bad ones.'

'You are reacting hostilely.'

'Do you like my brother?'

'I do not dislike him. Do you always pour drinks as strong as this?'

'It's a family trait. If you don't like him and you don't dislike him then you must have certain . . . reservations.'

133

'In the Special Branch we keep an eye on the weirdos, amongst other things. Lunatic left, irascible right and militant centres.'

'You're just playing with alliteration. I read the "Rhyme Of The Ancient Mariner" when I was fourteen. One cannot have a militant centre. Are you trying to tell me that John fits into one of these categories?'

'No. I was going to say that we pick up a bit of homespun psychology in the course of our duties and it strikes me that your brother must have had an unhappy childhood.'

'So he says. Father won't talk. Mother was an alcoholic and it wouldn't have taken a piano mover to push her over. John maintains that he was used as a go-between for both these conditions.'

'Don't you believe him?'

'I didn't say that. I was going to add that I was bundled off to a school in Switzerland which was as cold as the mountains around it.'

'Are you maintaining that you had as rough a time as he did?'

'Again, I didn't say that. But it certainly wasn't a laugh a minute. Look, let's get to the point, Kyle. Do you regard John as a threat to security, more particularly the security of Jack Steele?'

'No.' He paused and then added. 'Look. I am off duty. Steele is in Birmingham negotiating with Joe Mullins. I have no one to guard because he flatly refused to let me come along. I was bored. I had a lousy meal across the road and even worse wine and on an impulse I decided to visit the sister of a man I work with. Do you think you can grasp that and relax?'

There was a short silence during which he took their glasses over to the cabinet and refilled them.

'I'm sorry. I suppose I have been rather silly. But your appearance was unexpected and I know what you did to Holland. Perhaps I'm afraid of you.'

'I'll kill you later. Let's chat, first.'

She suddenly lost her edge and laughed. 'All right. What do you think of Jack Steele?'

'We might have made peace, but you're still turning this into a question and answer session. I like him.'

'He was here to dinner on Saturday. He seemed depressed half the time.'

'I've heard. Careless had been attacked. He knew that this thing with the General Workers Union was reaching the boil. Do you blame him?'

'I suppose not.'

Kyle surprised her by taking quite a different line. 'You have these holdings in Spain. Vast, I believe. With England a bob-sled out of control, careering down to her death, has it occurred to you to move house?'

She in turn surprised him with her answer. 'I move around a great deal, business-wise. London is purely a base. The Hacienda is so fully equipped that if I go there I do not even pack a case.' She shrugged. 'I know how bad things are, yet it is inconceivable to imagine England as a Communist country. Nevertheless if it happens I can transplant so easily. All I have to do is hop a plane.'

'Just make sure the seats aren't all sold,' Kyle said dryly.

She stared at him. 'Then you think that England has had it?'

'Unless something dramatic happens, and I can't imagine what. Tell me about this school of yours in Switzerland.'

'It was run by nuns. Get me another drink. The buildings were of stone. The nuns were German-speaking. They had stainless steel pumps inside them to circulate their blood. We call it a heart. Sometimes, when Father and Mother were going through a particularly bad patch, Frame would write to me and I would spend my school holidays there as well. Just me and the nuns. They kept silence at table and once when I broke it Mother Superior flogged me with a whip.' She jumped up suddenly, turned her back on him and pulled her jersey up so that he could see her bra-strap and eight fine light lines on the tanned skin. 'See them? They could have been worse but I heal well.' She turned back and he gave her the drink. 'That's the sort of thing the little bastard has never bothered to enquire about when he starts whining about his childhood.'

There was a short silence. Then she said, 'You're probably one of three people at the most who know. You'd better go, now. I've gone into a black mood and when it happens I can't get myself out of it for hours unless I get drunk. I don't want to get drunk because I've got an important assignment tomorrow.' She fleetingly touched the skin under her eyes. 'Already the make-up has to be put on more and more thickly.'

Kyle could see that she was serious. He stood up. 'That old bastard has a lot to answer for.'

'He's Prince Charming compared with some of the men I've met.' She sat down. 'They fall madly in love at first sight, and then dump me. *All* men are bastards.'

'Except me.' Kyle moved to the door.

'Why should you regard yourself as an exception?'

'Because I haven't fallen in love at first sight. In fact I think you're obnoxious. I'll pick you up at twelve thirty tomorrow for lunch.'

She stared at him and then unexpectedly laughed. 'God, Kyle, you are different.'

'So are you, Willoughby,' he said. 'See you tomorrow.'

'*Touché.* The name is Mary.'

'Ernest.'

'Now won't you go and play? If you've run out of toys I suggest the heavy traffic.'

'Okay. If I survive I'll see you tomorrow.' He flicked a hand, walked out of the apartment and softly shut the door.

XIV

It was very cold in the tiny cricket pavilion. Surprisingly, Mullins had brought only two of his muscle men and they remained aloof, bundled in coats and sharing a flask of coffee. Mullins himself gave every indication of being a man with a gigantic hangover and when he took off his coat and jacket, the way Steele had done at the opposite end of the changing room, he began immediately to shiver. To Bingham-Pope it was a strange state of affairs because

here we had Steele who, although he might have been constructed on burly lines, had not a spare ounce of lard on his frame, whereas Mullins carried probably seven stone of excess blubber, so that in effect it was the wrong man who shivered. He smelt strongly of liquor, though, and had obviously drunk long and hard through the night, so perhaps his ague was more one of stress than temperature, Once he was stripped down to pants and shirt he simply pointed out of the open doorway at the middle of the field where the pitch lay (he had said nothing to us by way of greeting, insult or any other means of communication since his arrival) and began to walk. Jack Steele followed him and told me later, when I enquired why the conference had been so short, what had happened.

They reached the pitch and Steele said idly, 'I should imagine that in the season this one would take a lot of spin.'

Mullins's teeth were chattering. He glared at Steele with

his bloodshot little eyes and said, 'We're not here to waste words. I want to tell you a few things. I got home last night and did some thinking. I also did some drinking. I considered my moral standards, such as they are, and decided that I could not be blackmailed into submission, the way it happened with the other Union leaders you broke. I decided that if I lost my wife and my little boy I had only myself to blame. When a man runs an affair he sticks his neck out and lays himself open to people like you. So I told my wife about Irma Saler and I told her about you.'

'That was pretty stupid,' Steele said, 'because I was going to give you the negatives. I used them only to get you to the conference table.' He looked down at the winter grass and added dryly, 'I mean the cricket pitch.'

Mullins was so surprised that he stopped shivering for a moment. 'Why? You had me over a barrel.'

'I don't like to work that way. I wanted to show you the error of your ways and then make a friend of you.'

Mullins stepped back and considered Steele. Then he shook his head. 'Whether you'd have given me the negatives or not would not have helped me.'

'What is your wife going to do?'

Mullins seemed confused by the question. 'It's none of your business but she's going to divorce me and apply for custody of the little chap. I will have the right of access to him at reasonable hours.'

'You are going to be surprised at her definition of "reasonable hours". If there is liquor on your breath, if you're a little late, you won't see the kid. She'll probably move to another city anyway. You've said goodbye to that kid.'

'Thanks to you!'

'No.' Steele shook his head. 'Thanks to Irma Saler and your own lusts.'

Mullins again appeared to consider while his whole body

138

shook. 'All right. Maybe so. But we're off the point, Steele. I'm here to tell you that there will be no negotiating. I'm here to tell you that I want my Union's pay demands met by noon tomorrow or you'll have on your hands the biggest strike this country has ever seen!' He began to lose control of himself and shouted. 'Now put that in your pipe and smoke it, Steele! I will cripple this country unless you change your mind and I don't care a damn for the consequences?'

'You should. It is your little boy who is going to starve. If we pay you what you want, the increase won't buy you a loaf of bread. The notes you will receive will be Monopoly money, just pretty things to play games with. If we turn you down, your strike will bring about the same situation. When England dies, Russia will attend the funeral.'

'You damn fool,' Mullins screamed. 'Don't you realize *that is what I want?*'

'Then there is nothing more to be said.' Steele's lips tightened and his eyes glittered. 'I talk no more with traitors.'

Mullins stared at him, panting, 'I'm no traitor!'

Steele moved up to him so quickly that he could smell liquor on the fat man's breath. 'You are so much of a traitor that in the old days you would have encountered the axeman's blade in the Tower. Now get away from here, you are polluting the air!'

Mullins began to turn around and then stopped. He said quickly, 'You'll be first on the scaffold,' and walked away at a pace surprisingly fast for a man of his weight.'*

Uncle was an old man with a white tonsure of hair, a gleaming, tanned pate, bright shrewd eyes and tobacco-stained teeth. He flicked over the last of the photographs of John Willoughby's diary and sighed and peered over the top of his

*See *Gird me with Steele,* supra, at page 271.

glasses at Dawson and Kyle who were sitting on the other side of his desk.

'What do you want to know?'

Kyle said, 'The issue of *Time* magazine. The hero-worship that has turned into hostility. The Field Marshal's uniform. His childhood which, if he is telling the truth, must have been incredible. His version of the manner in which his mother died – I don't know what it is but he has a version that differs from the Coroner's finding – the way he attaches significance both to Fox-Carrington's remark, "Turn the guns on London" and Fox-Carrington's death. He seems convinced that Clarke was responsible. I might add that the inquest has now been held and it was found that Fox-Carrington died of exposure after a huge alcohol intake.' He lit a cigarette. 'He talks of "undercurrents". He talks of there being a plot afoot. All this is building up to something in his mind. You're the mind specialist and we want to know what you think about Willoughby.'

Uncle said, 'Let's start off with his childhood and accept that he is telling the truth. He was lonely – his only companion appears to have been Frame, when the man was free, and that wasn't often – he was unloved and he was rejected. His mother was an alcoholic whore and his father an alcoholic satyr. Perfect foundation for what was going to happen to him later on. Then he had this affair as a young adult and was again rejected. Attempted his life, withdrew from society. Finally comes his last chance, the job with Jack Steele.' He stopped and began to pack his pipe.

'His reaction to Steele amounted to awe.' Dawson pulled a page of the diary towards him. 'Then one gets this sudden change of attitudes. Steele is "false" as he puts it.'

'You will probably find,' Uncle said, 'that without realizing it he came very close to falling in love with the man. Now he couldn't accept this, so his hostility was derived from a reaction formation against the homosexual wish. Thus, "I love him" became "I hate him" and this could have gone on –

because he didn't like the hate reaction either – into delusional thinking that Steele is plotting either to hurt him or others. Just what the plot is I don't know; all he says is that he is reaching a "conclusion". People like this are by nature extremely suspicious of everyone, having usually only one confidant, whom I presume in this case to be his sister. The slightest remark, a change of expression, a whisper that he cannot hear, is all about *him*. And, to cap it all, their thinking, although delusional, is surprisingly logical too, which is why they are often so hard to spot.' He took his time lighting his pipe. 'I wouldn't be surprised if he starts complaining of attempts on his life, soon. Ground glass in the turkey sandwiches. That sort of thing.'

'Is he a danger to security, more particularly Steele's?'

Uncle pondered. 'I don't think so. Certainly not yet. It all depends on this "conclusion". When it arrives and we know what it is, I will be able to tell you. Better keep an eye on him in the meantime. These people don't always resort to violence. Often they meddle and lay complaints and attempt to cause scandal. The so-called "poison pen" letters are an example. Sometimes they become great litigators. Did you burgle Steele's bedroom and check on the Field Marshal's uniform?'

'Yes, last night.' Kyle shook his head. 'Of course it wasn't there. There was no uniform of any kind.'

Uncle nodded. 'Well, there you are. He invented it to assist him in coming to this conclusion he talks about, although he personally would be convinced that it *is* there.'

Dawson said, 'You haven't put a name to him yet. You keep talking about "people like these". You seem to have classified him.'

Uncle puffed at his pipe. 'Sorry. I thought it would be obvious but then you're not psychiatrists. This chap is displaying decided paranoidal tendencies.'

They got up. Kyle said, 'Do you mean that he's a nutcase?'

Uncle winced and closed his eyes. 'I do wish you wouldn't

employ that kind of phraseology. What I mean is that he is demonstrating symptoms of a psychotic disorder involving delusions.'

'Then he's a nut-case in my book,' Kyle said, and walked out with Dawson.

Clarke was polishing an antique brass vase when Kyle came by. He straightened, cloth in hand. 'Been meaning to talk to you. Something's bothering me.'

Kyle stopped. 'I didn't fold my table napkin.'

'True. But it's not that at all. It's about Lord John Prick-Willoughby.'

The policeman's interest immediately quickened. 'Go on, I'm all ears.'

'Caught him red-handed on Friday coming out of the Boss's study. Now you know that nobody is allowed in there except on instructions, or if the Boss invites them in, with the exception of Mr Jenkins and Mr Hansom and of course Mr Bingham-Pope. The little squirt knows that too.'

Kyle was intrigued. 'Did he say what he was doing in there?'

'Borrowing a book. We had ... words, as they say.'

'Is that all he said? You know, by reason of who he is, he might not take the rule all that seriously. He might regard himself as privileged.'

'Oh, you bet he does. Except for one thing that alters matters.' Clarke fiddled with his polishing cloth. 'When the Boss bought this house he took over a lot of the furniture and loose items including the books in his study and the library. Some of them are priceless but the majority are worthless except that they *look* nice. We've got a catalogue that lists every volume.'

'What did he take?' Kyle asked softly.

'*A Manual On the Steam-driven Pump*, published in 1897.'

They regarded each other thoughtfully. 'On what day did this happen?'

'Last Friday.' Clarke paused and then added slowly, 'The

same afternoon that Tim got clobbered in the billiard room.'

'Have you told Mr Steele?'

'No. I didn't want anyone to think I was perpetually running off to him with tales. But I think he should know.'

'Yes, he should. Leave it to me.'

'Okay.' Clarke bent towards the vase and then straightened suddenly. 'There's another thing. I'm not afraid of a man just because he has a title. So I tore a strip off him and he told me not to speak to him that way. I told him to lodge a complaint with the boss if he saw fit and he said he was going to.' Clarke produced a small smile. 'But he hasn't.'

'I get you.' Kyle studied the burly young man with deep interest. 'You're a bright boy, Nobby.'

'I think so too,' Clarke said, and bent to his vase again.

When the telephone rang Beatrice Howard gave an exclamation of annoyance and rose to answer it. Her husband said impatiently, 'Let Jolly take it.'

'He went off ill just before you arrived home. I think the poor man has the 'flu.' She reached the instrument and lifted the receiver. 'Hello?' There was a short pause while she listened. 'No, we don't. My husband? He is a soldier.' There was another pause during which she became irritated. 'I frankly do not think that it is any of your business and you are grossly impertinent, but to get rid of you my husband is Brigadier Howard of the Fourth Armoured Brigade. Yes, tanks. Now will you kindly . . .' She put down the telephone and came back, slightly pink in the cheeks.

'Who the devil was that?' Kenneth Howard asked.

'Some ass wanting to know whether we use Kleenam Dishwasher. He said he was running a survey, and wanted to know your occupation.' She produced an embarrassed smile. 'I feel quite an ass, really, because just when I was about to ring off on him he rang off on me.'

'In future just put the 'phone down on that type. Kleenam Dishwasher, my God!' He stood up, a man of forty-five who could run ten miles with ease and bench-press his own body weight. 'Like a drink, dear?'

At the moment that Brigadier Howard was pouring whiskies for his wife and himself, Jack Steele stroked easily with his cue and a blue ball thumped into a pocket.

'Six. I'll take that red over there, bottom left pocket. Ahah!'

'Well played, sir! How did the P.M. take it?'

'Seven. Pink, top left pocket. He *wept*, Michael.'

'Senility? Oh, beautiful shot!'

'Thirteen. I'm not so sure. I think the old boy realizes that we failed and it's finished. This red over here. Because we did fail, didn't we Charles? There is not much more to be said.'

'I suppose so. Oh, bad luck, Jack!'

'It was a good try, wasn't it? I'm not concentrating properly though. How have things been while we were away?'

'All right except that Willoughby has become somewhat of a pain. Ernest knows about it.'

'What has young John been doing?'

'Snooping. Asking peculiar questions. Went into your study without permission to borrow a book. It is certain that he hasn't been got at or anything; he is doing it entirely on his own bat.'

'Why on earth?'

'I haven't the foggiest. He seems to be deteriorating. That white face and those shaky hands are getting me down.'

'Come on, it's your turn. Take this chap over here, it's a sitting duck. Is it not all brought about by his incredible nervous tension? Or are you implying that the lad is potentially dangerous?'

'Kyle says he isn't. Would you like to discharge him, sir?'

'Good shot! No, I don't think so, he's had a tough time and it would be rather unfair to dismiss the chap after so short a period of service. Let him settle, if he's going to. If he doesn't, we can ease him out gently after a while. What think you, Charles?'

'You're right, especially as long as he continues to invite us to dine with his sister. Gad but she's a looker!'

'It was a mistake to engage him, I must confess, but let's take the line that we're stuck with him and see how it goes. Bad luck, Michael. Now watch this.'

'Oh, shot! The blue?'

'No, I prefer the brown. What are the latest figures for the strike?'

'Just over a million, and still coming out. I don't know how you can be so cheerful, sir, I'm frightfully depressed.'

'I might appear cheerful, Michael. Inside, I am withering.'

Lord John Willoughby wrote in his diary for Wednesday:

I have made three serious mistakes. The first was when I asked Jenkins whether he had ever soldiered. He took note of the question. The second was my implication to Brixton that Fox-Carrington's death was no accident. And the third was the way I handled Clarke. He has been looking at me in a peculiar way. So has Kyle. So, for that matter, are all of General Steele's personnel. I must be far more circumspect about the way I handle this thing, if it is not already too late. I feel that they are on to something because of these errors and I must be more careful.

I learned only today that Kyle visited Mary. I am most disturbed about this move which I do not think was motivated by curiosity. Mary accepts Kyle's explanation because she has taken to him but I think he was there to see what he could find out. If only I could convince her that these people can now undoubtedly be classified as enemies whom, if they are desperate enough, might choose to do desperate things.

I have had a lot of bad luck with the telephone numbers I recorded from the back of Steele's appointment book. They seem to be largely home numbers and the owners are perpetually out. Results so far are:

Major General 'Fitz' Fitzmaurice, 5th Army Corps;
Sir Neville Mills-Manley, Ministry of Works;
Brigadier Kenneth Howard, Fourth Armoured Brigade;
Sir Richard Langley, Physician Superintendent of St George's Hospital, London;
Mr Tony North, News Editor of *The Times*.

While John Willoughby wrote, Kyle was seating Mary in Angelo's and considering the menu. 'It's nice to know that there are still some scampi around. What do you think?'

'I'll go along with that,' she said. 'And a salad.' She sipped the whisky he had bought her. 'By the way, the black mood has gone.'

'Three cheers.' Kyle took her hand. 'I have a sudden urge to kiss you, even if you are obnoxious. How does a Peer's daughter react to a kiss from a common copper?'

'It depends largely upon the kiss.' Her eyes were sparkling. 'Why don't you find out?'

'I will, after we've eaten,' Kyle said and turned to the wine list while she first glared at him and then laughed. On television at that moment a solemn-faced Prime Minister was telling the nation that talks between the Government and the Chairman of the General Workers Union had failed. At the same moment two men in overalls were admiring their handiwork in Mary's apartment. The older of the two went to the telephone, dialled and said merely, 'It's in. Now he can pour the wine over her head if he wants to.'

Kyle was brought a telephone at the table and a crisp feminine voice audible even to Mary, complained about her difficulty in tracking him down and then invited him to a party on Friday night. He turned it down regretfully on the grounds that he had a previous engagement.

'Popular chap, aren't you,' Mary observed. 'Who is your "previous engagement" – Princess Henrietta?'

Kyle smiled as he lit a cigarette. 'No, you.'

XV

If it wasn't the same helicopter that flew Lord John
Willoughby to the Missile Base in Northumberland on Thursday, it was just as draughty and was driven by the same pilot,
a dry man who seemed to have given up any idea of conversation because of the world of permanent noise in which he
lived. So John smoked and shivered, had a few nips from his
hip-flask when the pilot wasn't looking, and eventually
emerged stiff-kneed and freezing to be met by a bundled
soldier who was about as wide as he was high.

'Colonel heard you coming and sent me down to collect
you, Lord John. He's pleased with your timing, we've just
started our first drink. The name's Stoddart, by the way,
and because I'm the most junior subaltern I'm also the poor
fool who has to propose the toast tonight. You must be
experienced in this kind of thing. Do you think I should get
drunk or stay sober?'

John laughed. 'Can't you reach a happy medium?'

The young man shook his head. 'That's the trouble. I lose
my judgement so frightfully quickly. I think I'm sober when
in actual fact I'm not, so I just go on pouring. Disgusting
state of affairs.'

They had begun their ritual run from the helipad to the
Mess. Stoddart asked as they trotted along, 'Will Jack Steele
be able to come tonight? We'll be dreadfully disappointed if
he can't.'

'I've ... hardly ... seen him today.' John was already

blowing. 'The Cabinet was in session for . . . hours. It's this . . . Union thing.'

'Ah, yes. What those chaps need is a bayonet up the arse.'

They reached the Mess, its lights bright and welcoming in the darkness, and Stoddart showed him into a room blazing scarlet with the dress tunics of the officers. He blinked like an owl and found himself facing a smiling Brixton who held out his hand. 'Lord John! Welcome, lad! I believe there's still a chance that Jack might come. We've got the jet heli waiting for him just in case.' He threw a hard arm over John's shoulders. 'Here, come and meet the chaps.'

To John the officers seemed all alike – middle twenties to early thirties, pink-cheeked, physically very fit, relaxed and companionable, yet highly alert and functional. John found himself with Stoddart again. He said, 'I don't know if you remember, but I visited this place a few days ago. I had a copper with me, Jack Steele's bodyguard.'

'Oh, yes of course.' The subaltern had obviously opted for the unsober state and was drinking quickly, but he was so nervous that the whisky seemed to have very little effect. 'I didn't see you but I heard about your visit.'

'I was fascinated. Are you on standby at the moment?'

'We are mostly on standby,' Stoddart said. 'The day you chose was very rare indeed. At this moment the systems are alive and there are "volunteers" below in the silos. In addition six officers have to abstain tonight in case there's an emergency. Even the Colonel won't have more than two or three drinks. He never does unless he goes to Town for a blow-out.'

John shook his head in wonderment. He finished his drink and then heard Douglas Barraclough's rough call, 'Gentlemen to the table!'

John's place was at the top of two long tables arranged like a 'T' junction. He was next to Brixton on the C.O.'s left and there was an empty place on Brixton's right with a little card labelled 'J. E. Steele'.

148

The food came, and the wine. It seemed natural that they should be served roast beef and Yorkshire pudding, with roast potatoes and peas and gravy – an essentially English meal for English soldiers.

John found that he was surprisingly hungry. He kept pace with the best of them, later noting in his diary that

they seemed half starved until I realized that they were very fit men who expended hundreds of calories during each day. The mood was convivial throughout the meal, which ended with ice cream and hot chocolate sauce. The wine flowed and I noticed again that the Mess stewards were allowed the same liberties as Careless and Clarke. Then as soon as the coffee and port had been served an immediate silence fell. There were no cries of 'Shhhhh' such as one normally experiences. It was quite remarkable. Then Brixton rose with a full glass and said, 'Gentlemen, the King!'

'The King!' they responded. I felt that it was neither noisy nor enthusiastic.

Brixton seated himself again and let about fifteen minutes pass while the wine flowed on. Looking down the table at the scarlet uniforms, flushed faces and flashing eyes, I felt a moment of dreadful despair that I could not be as normal as they were, even if to be so I would have to accept the possibility of being consumed by the blast of a Drumhead missile.

Perhaps Brixton saw my momentarily downcast expression. In any event he nudged me and said, 'You're going to see something very interesting in a moment. I won't tell you beforehand because it will spoil everything, but listen carefully and charge your glass.'

Brixton rose to his feet amidst an absolute pandemonium of applause. He waited good-naturedly until it subsided and then said seven words. 'Mr Stoddart will now read the pledge.'

There was a complete hush while the young subaltern stood

up. He held some sheets of paper between fingers that trembled with nervousness despite his dogged intake of liquor. Most soldiers fear public speaking and he was no exception.

'Colonel, gentlemen. As you know, once every year this Regiment repeats a pledge made something like three hundred and thirty-five years ago. It arose at the Battle of Marston Moor and is best told in the words of a man who was there, and who set down the event in writing. That man was David Brixton, and as you also know the Brixtons have been Gunners ever since.' He gestured at the smiling Colonel and thunderous applause broke out while John stared dumbfounded at Philip Brixton who, in his 'history lesson' when John had first met him, had modestly not mentioned that his own family had started the tradition.

Stoddart was gaining confidence. He waited until silence had returned then put the first sheet of paper down on the table and began to read from the second.

'I greatly feared that the Royalists were going to win the day. Sir Thomas Fairfax's fellows on our right had been driven back by Lord George Goring. We had seen them break and flee and some of the men wished to abandon our cannon and follow suit. I took out my pistol and told them that the first man to leave his gun would be shot. In the centre a furious battle raged between the infantry and the Royalists' cries and cheers were very loud. We ourselves continued to bombard where we had been told, although it seemed of little purpose and we had very little powder remaining.'

At about this time I was on my way to tell the holders of the horse to be ready when an officer of the cavalry rode by. He was all bloody and his jacket slashed by sword-cuts. I knew him and asked him how it fared on our right and he said only, 'Leven and Fairfax have left the field, they believe it lost', and rode on.

I was filled with alarm because I knew the import of the

battle. I prayed silently for God's strong hand to guide us. Then a voice like the sound of a trumpet said, 'Have you gone to sleep on your feet, young man?' and I opened my eyes to see Oliver Cromwell looking at me while his cavalry came up behind.

'I was praying', I answered him, 'because I fear the battle lost. Leven and Fairfax have left the field.'

'But I have not,' he said in that voice of brass, and laughed. 'Do you fire at yonder ridge?'

'While we have the means,' I replied.

'The enemy are not there. You waste your time and my powder.' He stared down at me. 'I think I know thy father, lad, is thy name not Brixton?'

'It is, Sir. My father has a farm near St Ives, although I am a Master Gunner.' I pointed at my men, 'They are all farmers, here.'

'Farmers, indeed. A farmer cannot shoot a cannon straight, my boy, but he can ride, and it is cavalry I need to turn Goring, not those fire-breathing siege guns of thine. Come, all of you, take horse, take sword or sabre and form behind me!'

I then saw that he had many empty saddles in his ranks and that many of his men were begrimed and some were cut about the head or body. My men and I numbered all told three score and ten and all of us found mounts, and rode into the gap behind General Cromwell, whose trumpet voice all the time urged us to hurry.

When we were ready General Cromwell turned in his saddle and said to us, 'I'll have no unsteadiness, farmers. You do not know our usages so all I will tell you is that that way is forward' – and he pointed towards Goring's cavalry – 'and the other way is backward. Go forward all the time and you can do no wrong. Do you swear to be steady, before God?'

'We swear!' we cried, and with that we rode into battle.

I do not remember the fight clearly. But I remembered

to keep my eyes upon Cromwell for fear of doing something wrong. And when I enquired next day of my men they all said they had done the same.

When the charge was over, Cromwell rode towards us and stopped some distance away. He cried, 'That was a fine fight! Go back to those iron monsters of yours, whose use so far outshines their beauty. Well done, farmers!'

With that, he rode away with his cavalry and then I realized that the day was ours, and we had won the battle of Marston Moor.

Stoddart put the remaining papers on the table before him. 'There is little to add. We were cavalry for about three hours, I suppose, but it was an event unique in British military history. To this day, we use some cavalry terms and every year at this dinner we repeat our pledge and the toast we adopted after Cromwell came to rule England.' He picked up his glass. Everyone rose to their feet. 'Gentlemen, do you swear to be steady, before God?'

'We swear!' they thundered.

There was laughter and applause as the officers seated themselves again. Glasses were topped up. Brixton said smilingly to John, 'Well, what do you think of that? Do you think seventy farming folk turned the tide of battle?'

John was overwhelmed. 'It is amazing. The tradition itself . . . creates such . . . tremendous spirit!'

'I suppose that's why we do it, without really realizing it.' Brixton put down his cigar. 'I wish Jack had been able to come but it seems unlikely now.' He rose holding his glass. 'On your feet, gentlemen.'

There was a scrambling of chairs and somebody knocked over a glass. Then Brixton said, 'A toast, gentlemen.' He raised his glass high. 'The Lord Protector of England!'

'*The Lord Protector of England!*' they thundered. They saw the door open and Jack Steele's big figure stood there. He was smiling. They swung towards him. '*The Lord Pro-*

tector of England! The Lord Protector of England!' They followed him as he walked all the way across the mess to his place at the top table. *'The Lord Protector of England!'*

John Willoughby stared at the flushed faces, the mouths opening and closing like the mouths of puppets while all sound disappeared. He stared at the scarlet uniforms, the perspiration on healthy pink skins, the fists that began to pound the table in a rhythm. Of all those present, his was the only figure that was not animated, the only face that did not smile and shout, and his were the only eyes that did not flash fire. As he looked at Steele he seemed for a moment of time to be looking at a man in the uniform of a Field Marshal with the face of the devil, while Brixton beside him had assumed the expression of a hungry wolf.

Sound returned. Horseplay was starting. And Jack Steele was pounding him on the shoulder. 'Hello, young John! I so seldom see you that I forget you work for me. Enjoying yourself, lad?' His expression changed. 'What's the matter, John, you look ill!'

Lord John Willoughby said faintly, 'I . . . I'm . . . fine . . .' and then crashed to the floor. As darkness closed in he heard a bibulous voice saying, 'Whoops, first one to pass out!'

XVI

Mary Willoughby walked briskly between the piles of uncollected garbage from which arose a constant and worsening stench. She turned into her apartment building and did not bother to look for mail as the postmen had 'come out in sympathy'. She took the stairs because the lift wasn't working. There would be no electricity except for essential services.

She let herself into her flat, and closed the door; flipped her bag on to the sofa, and went into the kitchen to discover half a dozed unwashed glasses awaiting her attention.

She said, 'Oh damn,' because she had forgotten them; she was highly efficient and did not like to catch herself out. But she washed them quickly, put them on a tray nearby, and went back into the main body of the flat to place them in the old cabinet.

At this stage Mary tripped. It was nothing unusual – she often did so because she was a tall woman and not at all nimble. But this time she completely lost her balance and flung herself full length on the carpet, shrieking as she fell at the jangling death of six expensive glasses.

As she lay there grimly, unhurt but unhappy, she found that she was looking at an object no larger than a middle-sized button. It was so close to her nose that she pulled away to focus.

She opened her mouth to speak, thought better of it, and stared at the object, placed cleverly between the end of the wall to wall carpet and the skirting board, impossible to spot except for the kind of freak happening that had just taken place. At that moment there was the sound of John's key in the latch.

Mary said, 'Damnation, that's about fifty quids' worth of glasses gone west,' then got up quickly and ran quietly to the door, reaching it as it began to open. She saw her brother's white, startled face as she dragged him out into the passage and babbled, 'Oh John, thank God you're back! I've just broken six glasses and there's a hell of a mess to clean up, won't you buy us some cigarettes, there's only Hassan's open within a mile and they close in ten minutes.' All the while, she pointed alternately into the flat and at her lips until she saw his reluctant, uncertain nod.

He turned his back and went away while Mary ran back inside and busied herself with paper and a lipstick tube, so that by the time he returned there was a large notice just inside the front door. It read: THIS PLACE HAS BEEN BUGGED. KEEP CONVERSATION LIGHT UNTIL WE CAN GET OUT OF HERE.

She could see that, pale as he was, he had blanched. 'Hail brother. And thanks for the cigarettes. How was the Regimental Dinner?'

'It was magnificent,' he said as his sister pointed to the place where the bug lay. It was a foot or two from the old cabinet. 'Can I get you a drink?'

'Just one, Nora has bought the most delightful little puppy and I want you to see it. Let's have a quickie and then go next door.'

'All right.' John poured the drinks, then silently bent down to inspect the bug. Then he went back, gave his sister her glass, and perched on an arm of the sofa. 'Here you are.'

'Cheers. Tell me more about the dinner, I'm fascinated. Wild, I suppose?'

'Not really. Those chaps are frightfully fit and can take it. There was a bit of horseplay towards the end.'

'And the food?'

'Very nice, but plain. I don't suppose that it is the food that

155

counts so much as the *camaraderie*.' He was having great difficulty in sounding normal and she knew she would have to move him quickly.

'You don't look well. Finish that quickly and we'll have a look at the puppy. Then perhaps we can lunch somewhere, I haven't prepared a thing.'

'All right.' He threw back the remainder of his drink and headed for the door while she donned her coat, took her handbag off the sofa, and followed. She shut the door once they were outside, and grabbed his arm and roughly turned him so that he faced the wall.

'There are devices which can pick up speech if you're facing them. Now tell me, you bloody little bastard, what have you been doing that has got my flat bugged? Last time you bled all over the bathroom and nearly gave me a heart attack. Now it seems you're in some kind of trouble with the law!'

'I haven't done *anything!*' he said furiously. 'Nothing at all!'

She quivered with rage. 'Then why is my flat bugged?'

'I don't know!' He turned on her hotly. 'Perhaps it's you, going out with that confounded copper and saying something anti-government!'

She tried to control her rage. 'I never said anything more inflammatory than 'may I have another piece of the gateau.' Apart from which the Special Branch aren't political police yet, they don't bug one's flat because one says the government is incapable.'

He rubbed his face as though trying to restore life to dead flesh. 'Look. It's ridiculous standing out here fighting. Last night I tumbled to something which is so incredible that it hasn't left me all day and it may have some bearing on that bug in there. Let's go down to that frightful little pub on the corner, I have got to tell someone and I cannot trust anyone except you.'

She said worriedly, 'All right, John. Let me get my coat and some money.'

He waited while she re-entered the flat, snatched up her handbag and coat and said for the benefit of the bug, 'I don't know how the devil I could have forgotten my coat, hang on, I'm coming!' then walked with him briskly in silence down the stairs and along the street to 'The Glorious Twelfth', where she established herself at a booth while John bought the drinks.

There was no one on either side of them. In fact the tattered Victorian pub contained no more than a scattered handful of unsmiling patrons.

'Now what's it all about? What is this incredible thing you are talking about?'

'I must try and get the sequence of events in order.' He lit a cigarette with shaky hands. 'And I want to put my conclusion to you as a *fait accompli*, not just as my interpretation of events, because I am positive that I am right. First of all, when I first went to work for Jack Steele, I considered him a most incredible man, as you know. My admiration came very close to hero-worship. But it didn't take very long for me to realize that he is not only totally false but ruthless and calculating.'

'That's not a crime,' she observed. 'A lot of politicians fall into that category.'

'Maybe so, I don't deny it. But after about three days I sat down and reckoned with myself. There was a *Time* magazine profile on Steele that compared him with Cromwell and almost insinuated that he should be placed in a position of power. I found it in your flat, did you read it?'

I get magazines by the dozen. A lot are sent to me gratis if I appear in them, I certainly don't read them all.'

'Well I think that this ... started me off. It definitely brought to my notice that despite his resignation from the army, Steele is still essentially a military man. His household is organized on military lines. His staff are ex-army. He is constantly surrounded by officers of élite regiments. Why? Why is it necessary?'

'I suppose he misses the life.'

'Then why did he resign? Nobody forced him into it. In any event I decided to snoop around and see what I could find out, without really having any idea of what I was seeking. I did it all in the most hamhanded fashion but I was lucky.' He leaned forward, sweat beginning to break out on his forehead, 'Why should I discover the dress uniform of a Field Marshal hanging in his wardrobe? Unused, new, wrapped in a black plastic cover! Think about your answer while I get another drink.'

When he came back he said, 'Why? Come on, I want your opinion.'

She stared at him as though mesmerized. 'Are you absolutely positive?'

'Entirely. I saw it. I examined it.'

'Well, then . . . I suppose because he proposed to wear it . . . isn't that the logical answer?'

'It's logical, yet Steele never rose higher than Lieutenant General.' His face twisted as it glittered with perspiration. 'So what is the conclusion in this instance?'

She said hesitantly, 'That he . . . he proposed to return to the army and . . . and attain higher rank?'

'Precisely. What is more, rank that had been guaranteed. A private soldier does not order his corporal's stripes until he has been told he's promoted.' He went on to tell her briefly about Careless's arrival and what he had done. 'I was in a state of complete distress. I even thought I might have killed him. Then when I got back from my visit to father I heard that Kyle had attributed the attack to a prowler who had broken the pantry window. The window might have been broken beforehand, and misled Kyle. But I doubt it. He is most astute. It has been worrying me that he might have covered up for reasons I don't know.'

'He might be working on the "give a man enough rope" principle if he suspected that a member of the household had done it. That's his job.'

John Willoughby scrubbed the sweat off his forehead with an impatient forearm. 'It may sound strange but I rather hope so. It would explain the bug, which is worrying, but also indicate that he has everyone under surveillance. In other words, everyone is bugged or followed. Kyle is worried. Someone within the household attacked Careless for a reason other than burglary. It is this that has set him off.' He drank deeply again. 'Now we come to the night of your dinner party. You are aware of the fact that Fox-Carrington got abominably drunk. But while you were in the kitchen helping Clarke he said something that seemed most significant. Steele, Bingham-Pope and Brixton all reacted most coldly and hostilely. Fox-Carrington was pulling Brixton's leg about the . . . the awful death-dealing potential he has in those Drumheads he sits on up north. He was doing it in a drunken sort of way. Then he said that for all Brixton knew, he might at any moment be called upon to "turn the guns on Moscow".' He swatted sweat again, his feverish eyes never leaving his sister. 'They didn't seem to like this . . . this phrase. Bingham-Pope tried to shut him up. Brixton was angry. But he just went on while they froze. He was too far gone to listen. He went on to suggest that Brixton might have to turn his missiles – he always used the old-fashioned word "guns" – on China, and then finally . . . finally he said who knew when Brixton might be ordered to "turn the guns on *London?*" He said it in an especially meaningful way.'

Mary's lips shone with the wetness of her drink. 'Do you mean as though it had a double meaning?'

'Yes. He then turned to Steele as though he'd had a moment of insight into what he had done and admitted that he was drunk. Steele resorted to archaic phraseology, the way he so often does. He did not look at Fox-Carrington. He just told him to leave the table and get out and Fox-Carrington obeyed. You came back from the kitchen at that stage.'

'I noticed the tension. But Clarke had walked out without a

word and I was having difficulty coping although I tried not to show it.'

'The next day Fox-Carrington was found dead behind a hedge in a square just off Belgravia.'

She let the silence run. 'Are you trying to tell me that Nigel was . . . murdered?'

'Yes.' He stubbed out his cigarette and lit another. 'Yes, I am. By Clarke. All he had to do was catch up with Nigel Fox-Carrington, lead him behind the hedge and wait until he passed out. It would not have taken long. Minutes, maybe. The rest was up to nature, that cold night.'

She shivered abruptly, as though turned cold by the thought of it, and took up her drink. 'John, you have no proof of all this.'

'Wait.' He made a placating gesture. 'Just wait, I am now in a position where I have an ex-army man who has resigned from the military and devoted his life to politics. Yet this man spends all his time with apparently devoted officers of, as I have said, élite regiments. He has a Field Marshal's uniform in his cupboard and when one of his henchmen slips up he is found dead the next day. Then, with a reputation of accomplishing the impossible as far as strike-breaking is concerned, he fails with Mullins. A day later I attend the Regimental Dinner of his best friend, Brixton, and a surprising thing arises. It transpires that one of Brixton's ancestors who was a Master Gunner was pressed with his men by Oliver Cromwell into abandoning their cannon and acting as cavalry for a very short time, a matter of hours during the battle of Marston Moor. Before the fighting started, Cromwell made them swear "before God", as it was put, that they would be "steady". Every year they repeat this pledge. And then, by tradition, a toast is made to this man they so admired, using the title Cromwell assumed after Charles's death, when he assumed power. They drink a toast to "The Lord Protector of England!" '

He stopped for a moment, staring at her hypnotically. 'The

Mess door flew open and there stood Jack Steele, grinning like the devil. And they carried on shouting. *"The Lord Protector of England!"* they cried as he walked the length of the room. *"The Lord Protector of England!"* It went on and on and then I knew that very soon Jack Steele would take over the reins of government as Despot. Then I fainted.'

Again, he was breathing so fast that he suddenly thought he might pass out. He got up quickly and bought two more whiskies.

'John.' She leaned across and took his hand. 'If you are right. If, mind. When will this take place?'

'Very soon. I think Steele and his supporters regarded the negotiations with Mullins as the final test. Steele had hoped to break Mullins like he broke the others. He appreciated that he might fail, though. And if he did, then he would act. The code word to Brixton up in Northumberland would be *Turn the guns on London,* which is why Fox-Carrington lost his life for letting it slip. A Drumhead 2 missile, carrying a conventional warhead, is so accurate that it can be dropped on an area the size of a small carpet. The target this time would be Parliament while in session, surrounded by Zed-Force. The members would have the option of either handing over the reins of government to Steele, or be destroyed inside the building, or be shot as they emerged.'

She thought for a moment. 'What are you going to do? Are you going to report this to someone?'

He said more slowly, and with deeper deliberation, 'Mary, this is essentially a rebellion of the right, although Steele will find more support than anyone expected amongst the blue collars and the working classes. Nevertheless, I am confident that Steele would never move unless he had all law-enforcement bodies and the armed forces committed to him.' He ticked them slowly off on his fingers. 'The Commissioner of Police. Zed-Force's Colin Campbell. Civilian and Military Intelligence. All the top people with any power at all at Whitehall. To whom would I go without fear that they are themselves involved?' He shook his head. 'I would disappear into Work Force without a sound and never come out again.'

'The Press? What about them?'

He hesitated. 'I don't think so. They have very limited powers of publication as it is and this thing is so mind-blowing that they would demand proof – all these people would demand proof, and *I haven't really got it.* They're going to say, "How can we publish speculation and be ruined in a mammoth libel suit and prosecuted by the Government to boot?" '

'They have the means to investigate, surely.'

'In their fashion. But how long would it take them? I just do not know what to do! Do . . . you believe me?'

She said seriously, 'Yes. But only because I know you and can trust you.' There was a short, worried silence into which she said, 'John, have you considered the possibility that what Steele might intend doing is right? I mean, that if by becoming a . . . Dictator, I suppose one would call it, he were to put Britain back on her feet . . . wouldn't that be a good thing?'

His face tightened with feeling. 'Never! England lives or dies by Democracy *and nothing else!'*

'Be quiet!' she said sharply. 'People are looking.'

He lowered his voice but it shook with feeling. 'At the moment we are still coping. We are keeping our heads above water. The Unions must see sense in the long run. We might have to go hungry but we are the last of the true Democracies and if we have to slide into ruin as a Democracy, so be it. There must never be any other form of rule in this beloved Britain.'

'All right. I know your standards and I accept them. In fact I agree with you. Thank God we always have the Hacienda to fall back on.'

He said nothing, and in silence they ate meagrely, speaking very little, but as they left the pub she stopped suddenly and grabbed John's arm. 'I know whom you can see. Someone totally above suspicion.'

162

He regarded her wonderingly. 'Who would that be?'

'The King,' she said flatly.

An hour later North took off his earphones and flicked a switch and said to Carter, 'I tell you, they've seen that bug. When she fell with that tray of glasses she damn nearly blew out my eardrums. She must have been a foot away from it. Their conversation at the moment is so stilted it sounds like a very bad play. You know how people sound when they're putting on.'

Carter shrugged. 'I've got an idea that will tell us for sure.' He went to a telephone, dialled, spoke for a while, then hung up. North went back to his listening.

Half an hour later the telephone shrilled. Carter rushed to it and listened carefully. Then he put it down and looked at North dispassionately. 'There is no "Nora" next door. The neighbours are only on good morning terms with Mary and John. And there isn't any puppy, either. In fact they're not allowed in the building.'

North took up the phone. 'I wonder if Ernest feels like a little more burglary?'

The King was in a decidedly snappish mood and he made no attempt to disguise the fact. 'I only agreed to see you because I've known you and your family for so many years. Now, John, what is all this about "life and death" and all the other alarming phrases you employed to get in here? I'm leaving early tomorrow and I am hardly ready.' He glared at John expectantly.

John tried to control his trembling, hoping that the tranquillizer he had taken thirty minutes before would soon have its effect. 'Sir, I believe this country to be in desperate danger.'

'Of course it's in danger! We're in a hell of a mess, quite frankly. Is that all you came to tell me?'

'No, that isn't what I meant.' He fiddled around frantically but could not smoke because his Sovereign was an arch enemy of tobacco. 'I believe that very soon, maybe within a few days, a military *coup d'état* will take place. Sir, I must beg you to keep this between the two of us, until you decide what to do. High officials in all departments of this country's government are involved. That is why I came to see you, because I could not safely speak to anyone else.'

'You had better be damned careful what you say.' His Majesty's piercing eyes bored into those of the shaky-handed young man. 'You are talking of sedition!'

'I know I am.' John did not flinch.

'Then go on. There is no recorder in this room and as far as the outside world is concerned you have called to . . . to wish me *bon voyage.*'

John spoke for twenty minutes. At the end of it the King said, 'You know of course that this kind of thing has been mooted – sometimes quite openly – for years. Usually by retired bumbling old Colonel Blimps who had no intention of really doing anything. What you're saying is of course quite different. You are saying that we have it virtually in our laps.'

John said dry-mouthed, 'Yes, I am, Sir, and I adhere to it.'

'Oh, I can see your conviction. I admire you for your pluck in coming here.'

John said nervously, 'Do you believe me?'

The King got up and began to pace his study. 'No, I don't.' The words came as though with the snap of steel doors shutting. 'Do you want to know why, John? It is because any *coup d'état,* be it from the left or the right, has to involve deposing *me.* There is no way around it. They are *obliged* to depose the Monarch. So therefore I take the line that I am cognisant of nothing. I hear nothing and I see nothing from either side. You have not spoken to me and I have not spoken to you about anything other than trivialities.'

John arose, weak-kneed, weary and dejected. 'I think they will depose you, Sir. Or at the least you will not be allowed back to England for some years, and then only on their terms.'

The King stopped his striding. 'Drop this thing, John. You have no facts, no proof, no evidence. You have a very unfortunate personal background. Only disaster can come of what you are attempting.'

'I cannot.' John moved to the door. 'May I wish you a most pleasant holiday, Sir.'

XVII

Extract from the final entry in the diary of Lord John Willoughby, second son of the Duke of Narsham, for Friday.

The King rejected me.

At first I hated him for it. But no longer. I am writing this in mid-afternoon after experiencing a most strange happening which I would like to put on paper while it is still fresh in my mind.

My footsteps dragged homewards. My Sovereign, the one person I thought might believe me, had turned me down. I did not want to take a taxi or a tube. I walked.

The flat seemed to enclose me, Mary had gone somewhere. I poured a drink and reflected on the fact that I had no one left to turn to. I began to weep because although England was not yet dead she was on her deathbed. I was attending the last rites of Democracy. So I put my hands together and raised them to Heaven while I fell on my bended knees and prayed for the salvation of my country.

Nothing happened for a while. Then in a sudden blinding flash God appeared and filled me with greatness. I was transported, I was taken on high to see the ruined towns and cities of so many countries. I was permitted to see nations destroying themselves in civil war.

And then came peace and joy. A joy I had never known before. I was infused with it because I now knew exactly what to do. This discovery transcended everything and would bring peace to my country forever. I was not at all afraid of what I had been appointed to do. Suddenly my mind has the clarity of a bell. As soon as I have put down my pen I shall take a taxi to Waterloo. My first step is to visit Father.

Kyle said in a worried way, 'After the bug failed because of Mary's freak accident I was compelled to burgle again this afternoon while Mary was out and her crazy brother was seeing His Majesty. I found a couple of things, but this in particular will interest you.' He handed over more hurriedly-processed copies of pages out of John Willoughby's diary. 'Read these.'

Uncle took them and read ponderously while Kyle fidgeted. It seemed hours before he looked up and peered at Kyle over the top of his spectacles. 'He has gone all the way now. He has reached his conclusion and in his own mind is firmly convinced that he has been ordained by God to carry out a mission to save his country.'

'What is the conclusion?'

'Don't you know? It's obvious.'

'I want to hear it from you.'

Uncle sighed. 'It is that General Steele proposes to become the second Lord High Protector of England.'

'And what does Willoughby feel ordained to do?'

'To assassinate him. You will have to act quickly.'

'I intend to.' Kyle got up. 'Is John Willoughby now insane?'

'To employ layman's language for once,' Uncle said sadly, 'he is as mad as a hatter.'

The Canadian killer, Charles Holland, sat in the library of the house in Belgravia with a book on his lap which he had been reading from time to time. It was *Hereward The Wake* and although he had been enjoying it he had been interrupted by other thoughts that demanded his attention.

He was not discontented. Steele refused to have him in his company and Campbell had so far steadfastly refused to replace him, so that Holland was being highly paid for doing nothing. All that bothered the hit-man was the terrible hatred of Steele that he nursed like a wound in his feline intestines, and after Steele there was Kyle.

So he sat in the quiet of the library and plotted, deciding that as soon as he had accomplished what was in his mind he would return to Canada. But not until then.

Jack Steele stared angrily at the cars, trucks and uniformed men in front of his house and said, 'What the devil is going on here?'

'I will tell you inside.' Kyle led the way through the milling crowd of policemen. Clarke, watching from within, saw them coming and opened the door as they arrived.

In the drawing-room Steele still steamed. He said severely, 'Ernest, I do not like being kept in the dark and I do not like a bunch of coppers turning my house into a menagerie. You had better have a damned good reason for dragging me back from the House in the middle of an important debate and assembling us here.' He looked to the window where darkness was falling. 'Make it quick, I have a great deal to do.'

Kyle said urgently: 'I had to get you here together because it is imperative that you all hear what I have to say.'

He regarded Steele, and Bingham-Pope, Careless, Jenkins and Clarke with a feeling that he had failed somewhere. 'John Willoughby is insane. This has been confirmed by a psychiatrist. He is a paranoiac, which means that he suffers from a psychotic disorder accompanied by delusions. The delusion in his case is you, sir. He sincerely believes that within a matter of days you intend to overthrow the government of this country by military *coup d'état* and rule as Dictator, or as he puts it, the second Lord Protector of England.'

Steele stared at Kyle for a long moment. 'Are you mad, mad? That's absurd!'

'I am afraid that it is John Willoughby who is mad,' Kyle said quietly. 'And there is more to it. He believes that he has been ordained by God to assassinate you and thereby save Democracy. We have it all from his diary in black and white. There is no element of doubt in this. The diagnosis was made by Sir Howard Fuller, of whom you have no doubt heard.' He crossed to the television set. 'I appreciate how impossible all this sounds but you will have to learn to accept it.'

He pressed the 'on' switch and the screen came alive to show a bespectacled newscaster finishing an item about a ferry disaster in Burma. Then the man squared his shoulders and adopted a solemn mien. 'We have been asked by the London Metropolitan Police and the Commandant of Zed-Force to request the public's assistance in a matter of enormous importance which could involve loss of life. To this end the police wish to interview Lord John Willoughby who might be able to assist them in their enquiries. Anyone knowing the whereabouts of Lord John Willoughby should immediately contact their nearest Police Station or the Headquarters of Zed-Force or telephone the following numbers.' He gave three numbers, repeating each in turn, while a slightly blurred black-and-white photograph of John appeared on the screen. Then the picture went off and the newscaster returned. 'The official description of Lord John Willoughby is as follows; height, five feet nine inches. Weight, ten stone. Build, slim. Colour of hair light brown, colour of eyes grey. General appearance neat and good-looking, manner extremely nervous and inclined to stammer. This message will be repeated every half hour on all stations.'

Kyle switched off and the screen went black. 'He has disappeared from his sister's flat and we do not know where he is. Now do you believe me?'

'Yes. By God, it's hard. I liked the boy.' Steele seemed to consider. 'Want us to stay put, eh?'

'I do, sir. The police outside are being reinforced by Zed-Force at the moment. Enormous efforts are being made to apprehend Willoughby but we cannot take any chances with a man who has stalked and outwitted the great cats in their own jungles.'

Bingham-Pope said abrasively,' 'I suppose you realize, Kyle, that all this would never have come about if the Special Branch had not declared Willoughby fit for employment.'

'We never declared him fit,' Kyle responded sharply, ignoring Jenkins's noisy support of Bingham-Pope. 'His own psychiatrist did, when the man must even then have been exhibiting paranoidal tendencies.' He stopped suddenly as though gripped by a sudden new thought, then went on. 'In any case, is it necessary now to play "I told you so"?'

'Yes.' Steele regarded Kyle thoughtfully. 'I agree. We can save the recriminations for later although I too think that your department slipped, Ernest. Now you talk about a diary. How did you get hold of it?'

'I burgled his flat twice, the last time a mere few hours ago.'

'Then you must have been suspicious, surely, to do a thing like that. Why did you not warn me?'

'Because on the first occasion the diary contained no threat of violence. Our own psychiatrist felt that he had no evidence to justify my asking you to discharge Willoughby. Apart from which your standing orders have always been that where we suspect an attempt is going to be made we are to take precautions to protect you but let the attempt go ahead. I think I *have* warned you, now that the second burgling revealed a categorical decision to attempt your life.'

Steele mulled this over. 'Fair enough. How did you get on to the chap in the first place?'

'A chance remark he made about a story on you in *Time* magazine. This story does not exist. It was the beginning of his deluded thinking.'

'I remember that incident,' Jenkins said suddenly, now looking at Kyle with approval.

Steele said to Clarke, 'Nobby, bring us some drinks, I

think we all need one.' Then he turned to Kyle. 'What do you want us to do?'

'Stay here until we get him.' Kyle pointed to a briefcase he had placed on a table. 'I am authorized to arm you if you have no weapons. There are six fully loaded 9mm Walthers in that case if you want them.' He looked at his watch. 'I have to leave for a while. Campbell will be joining you shortly with a radio and I will be back later. Personally I don't think that you will need the guns but I will leave them with you.'

'I'll stick to my Holland and Holland,' Steele said, once more the imperturbable English gentleman.

John reached his father's estate in a stolen motor car ten minutes before the first alarm went out on television. He skidded to a halt and trotted up the steps of the great old house leaving the car's motor running. He did not knock but simply opened the door and walked in.

There was no one in the hall but he could hear loud voices and laughter from the drawing-room. The Duke was entertaining again.

John walked quickly and silently to the gunroom, locking the door behind him and going straight to the rack. His breathing was even and he no longer trembled. Without any hesitation he took down a strange-looking weapon, a rifle with a pistol grip as well as a stock. From a drawer below he brought out two boxes of ammunition and two twenty-shot clips which he filled with the speed of an expert. He slapped one into position just ahead of the trigger-guard and put the other in a trouser pocket. From another drawer he took a Smith and Wesson Combat revolver, loaded it with .308 Specials and jammed it into the waistband of his trousers.

Returning to the hall he headed for the main telephone, grabbed the cable and ripped it loose from the instrument. With the main phone out of action, none of the extensions could dial out.

He looked around, checking, then went quickly to the

drawing-room and stood in the doorway holding the rifle across his chest. 'Good evening, Father.'

One by one, startled, they looked around. With the exception of Swanby, who was carrying a tray of drinks, and the angelic-faced Carol, the eight remaining guests were elderly.

The Duke of Narsham got up. 'My dear boy, what an unexpected surpwise! What on earth do you want the wifle for at night? Going to give us an exhibition?'

One or two of the guests tittered nervously. There was a look about the young man that had made all of them uneasy.

'I'll tell you in a moment. But first, has Frame left yet?'

'Yes, the bastard! Walked out on me with his whole family after all these years and I've got a shoot next Saturday.' They were speaking across the whole length of the drawing-room, The Duke's voice came again, a little uncertainly. 'Why the wifle, John?'

'Frame told me about Mother's death. He told me I was right.'

The Duke raised his podgy little hands. 'Fwame hated me! He's lying!'

John looked towards the guests. 'He took my mother to the Coach and Pair one night and got drunk. It had been sleeting and the roads were very slippery. On the way back he lost control at a bend and the car rolled. He was unhurt but he could see that Mother was dying. He knew that he would face a charge of manslaughter because he had boasted to people at the Inn that he intended to "break the record" going home. Some of them even begged him not to drive. Furthermore it was most unusual for him to drive at all, he invariably had the chauffeur, on top of which he had made so many drunken threats against her life over the years that there was a strong chance he might even be charged with murder.'

'John my boy, that's untwue . . .'

'Shut up,' John said dispassionately. 'The car was lying on its right side. He had my Mother virtually on top of him. But he managed to push her off and then got out by climbing up through the left side door which he left hanging open. When the first motorist arrived, my mother was in the driving position and my father told him that my mother had in fact been driving. He repeated this statement to the police, later, maintaining that he'd had second thoughts about driving when he left the Inn, and allowed her to take the wheel. My mother died on the way to hospital.'

'Please, John, my deah fellow, give me a chance to explain . . .'

'There is nothing to explain.' John lifted the rifle to his shoulder and fired in almost the same moment. His father's shriek overrode the sound of the second shot that took Swanby in the chest and smashed him over backwards in the very act of hurling the tray at John.

There was a silence broken by his father's moans; he lay on the floor with blood seeping through his trousers at the crutch. Swanby was dead.

John studied his father quite expressionlessly. 'There's poetic justice for you.' Then his features twisted and he laughed abruptly and shrilly. 'All of you remain here. The telephone is out of action. If one of you moves, I'll put a bullet in him.' Then he turned and walked out, locking the front door and pitching the key into the darkness. He stared at the stolen car which was still idling in neutral, then shook his head and turned to the garage; the engine of the Rolls burst easily into life under the twist of his fingers. Tyres shrieked as he reversed out, then slammed the car into forward gear and roared down the road. At the entrance to the estate he turned right and watched the speedometer needle move over the eighty mark as he thundered towards London.

Mary Willoughby opened the door to her flat and cried, 'Oh Ernest! It's good to see you! Has he been found?'

'Not yet.' Kyle shut the door. 'But he will be. We are not dealing with a man who wants to escape. We are dealing with a man who wants to attack. He must come to us.'

She said only, 'Would you like something to drink?'

'Yes, please. Whisky.'

'Coming up. I've been so desperately worried. And every time I switch on the television it gets more alarming.' She returned with the drinks. 'You look tired.'

'Thanks. I am. I've been a busy little bee. A copper's life is strange. Somebody said something to me only a few hours ago and I suddenly realised how blind I had been. I went straight to a villain and told him that I knew all, and arrested him. He immediately began to sing like a canary, and his song led me to another villain whom I also arrested. My day is nearly done. Cheers.'

'Cheers.' She lit two cigarettes and gave him one. 'All this work. Long hours. Is it worth the salary you are paid?'

'Not really. But there are rewarding moments like today when one wraps up something big.' He fiddled in the inside pocket of his jacket and produced a plain white envelope. 'Consequently, I am feeling expansive. I have a present for you. Here you are, with my love, even if you are obnoxious.'

She laughed. Her eyes sparkled. 'Ernest! What on earth!' She ripped the envelope apart and then her smile died and she regarded him puzzledly. 'An air ticket to Spain!' The smile began again, curving the corners of her ruby-red lips. 'Are you propositioning me?'

'No, there is only the one ticket.' He sipped his drink, looking at her with deep interest.

She had gone straight-faced on him. Slowly she said, 'Why, Ernest?'

'Because of this,' Kyle said, and she found herself looking at the *Time* magazine issue with the picture of Jack Steele on the cover. 'It is a brilliant piece of work. Could fool anyone. Henry Greer at Contra Studios should get some sort of prize instead of getting the jail cell in which he is at present languishing.' Kyle smiled. 'Incidentally, he has a cell-mate, a leading Harley Street psychiatrist by the name of Bertram Lomax.'

174

She seemed thrown into confusion, not knowing which subject to deal with first. But the issue of *Time* seemed to fascinate her. 'Where did you get this . . . this . . .'

'I burgled this flat three times. On the first two occasions I was concerned entirely with your brother and his diary. The last time was a quickie, not more than an hour or two ago, and it didn't take long because I had been told where to look.' He regarded her with mocking disapproval. 'You would have been far better advised to have burnt it once it had served its purpose, you know.'

All the colour had drained out of her face. She whispered, 'How did you . . .'

'Find out?' Kyle stood up holding his glass, so that he could look directly into her face. 'Today I was very ashamed of myself and considered myself a very bad copper for being so unobservant. I was also blinded by your beauty. Now, in retrospect, I don't think I have done too badly because I put it all together in time. I was telling Jack Steele and his entourage that your brother is a homicidal maniac who is in the process of making an attempt on Steele's life. Charles Bingham-Pope quite rightly attacked me for passing John as fit for employment. I became annoyed and told him that it was John's own psychiatrist who had done the passing, not me. I then realized somewhat tardily that Lomax had stuck his neck out very, very far in doing this. He must have known at the time John was exhibiting paranoidal tendencies yet he concealed his knowledge. There was also the fact that when John saw the *Time* story he still liked and admired Steele. Repression of the latent homosexual desire had not yet occurred, so it was unlikely that John's delusional thinking started at that stage. I went straight to Lomax and told him that I knew he had been used. I took a chance and arrested him and he broke down. He was the first of the two villains I mentioned when I arrived here. His song led me on to Henry Greer.'

Kyle regarded her sorrowfully. He lit a cigarette while she

retreated slowly and wordlessly, eventually coming up against the far wall where she flattened herself against it in a strange position as though the wall offered her security.

'I don't know what you're talking about.' Her eyes glittered.

'Oh yes you do. You masterminded this operation quite brilliantly. The only trouble is that you are more cracked than your brother.'

'Get out of here!' she shouted suddenly, not moving, transfixed to the wall.

'Only when I have finished my drink.' Kyle sipped again. 'God knows, I need it. Do you know, I genuinely believed you when you told me that every man you met dumped you. But you were only half right. There were other lovers who became your faithful slaves, the ugly ones like Lomax and Greer who were prepared to risk their careers for you. You were right, though, that there were some men to whom you were fatally attracted and who belonged to the love-'em-and-leave-'em brigade. Like Jack Steele. Correct?'

She said nothing, flattened against the wall as though it were the impenetrable exterior of a womb she wished to enter.

'You had the baby in October,' Kyle said, 'by which time Steele was finished with you. When I saw in Sarah Brixton's baby a carbon copy of Steele, I was very confused. When I visited you, and saw as much of you in the child as Steele, I was dumbfounded. I could not take my thinking any further. Now, of course, it's easy. Hell hath no fury like a woman scorned, especially one who has to give up her infant because no scandal dare attach itself to the life of a Cabinet Minister in a shaky government. You developed a hatred of Steele far greater than your hatred of your brother who had stayed at home while you languished in a convent staffed by mad sadistic nuns.' Kyle pointed up at the rows of books on their shelves. 'I missed those, the first two times. I was concerned purely with John. But the third time Lomax told me what to look for. There must be a dozen of them, every one on abnormal psychology. You wanted your revenge on Jack Steele but you weren't prepared to risk your pretty little neck. Why not convenient John, who was also born a stalker and a marksman? Perfect for the choice. All he needed was motivation. So you worked out your little plan, got it okayed in principle by Lomax who could not guarantee success but thought it likely, and then made "friends" with Steele, while at the same time forcing him, with a mild little piece of social blackmail, to engage your brother.'

She said again, pressed against the wall, still trying to force entry, 'I do not know what you are talking about.'

'Oh yes you do.' Kyle shrugged. 'It worked. Congratulations. You might have a dead Steele to show for it but you'll more likely have a dead brother.' He consulted his watch. 'You had better hurry, your flight leaves in just over an hour and I know you don't have to pack. Go back to Miguel, poor simple bastard that he must be. And by the way, if you turn this offer down, I'll be back – but my present will be different – a pair of linked bracelets.'

For the first time her head moved. It came round little by little. Her eyes still glittered but held a note of curiosity. 'Why are you letting me go?'

Kyle dropped his hands. 'Because you are just too damned beautiful to go to jail. Thank your Creator for your good luck.' He turned away with his eyes on the mirror and ducked suddenly as a plate shattered above his head. 'Killing me wouldn't really have helped, you know; Lomax and Greer are still singing in harmony. Goodbye, Mary. *Hasta la vista.*'

The Rolls was doing a hundred miles an hour when John Willoughby saw the road block. It was at the very furthest range of his powerful headlights so he had the time to slow down and see the Zed-Force truck parked on the verge and the four Zed-Force troopers standing near it, their head- and body-armour making them look like aliens from another world.

The road block was too stoutly constructed to break and the Zed-Force troopers would have made short work of him with their Stens in the soft-skinned car. So John pulled to a halt twenty yards away and left his lights on. He got out and put the Cetme to his shoulder just as they began to waddle forward. He heard one cry, 'Look out, that's . . .' then squeezed the trigger four times in less than four seconds and watched them tumble and sprawl. He had aimed for the throat and been dead accurate with three of his shots but the fourth man had taken the bullet high up on the chest and although his armour had prevented the bullet from penetrating, he was on his knees, head down, gasping from the impact. John put another bullet through the top of his head and the trooper fell over soundlessly on his side.

John ran back to the Rolls and extinguished its lights. Then, working with incredible but methodical speed, he stripped off his trousers, jacket, shirt and shoes, paused for a moment to measure the bodies with a careful eye and then stripped the one closest to his size, donning the man's boots, battledress, armour and gas-mask.

The keys to the Zed-Force truck were in the ignition. The truck started at once and he turned it in a tight curve and headed onwards for London.

Dawson and Kyle were standing outside Steele's house in Belgravia where police and Zed-Force troopers milled. Dome lights flashed and there was a coming and going of men and machines. Police dogs barked savagely from their mesh-enclosed cage on the back of a truck.

A sergeant came pushing his way through to them. 'Radio, sir. My car. I'll show you the way.'

Dawson left with the Sergeant and came back after only a few minutes. His face was grey with strain. 'My God, Ernest, the man is now quite crazy. He has been out to his father's estate. Killed his older brother and maimed the Duke, who may die. He's in agony. Then he took the Rolls and is believed to be heading back for London.'

Kyle said, 'I'd better go inside and tell them.' He turned away and then stopped and swung back. 'What do you mean, the Duke was maimed?'

Dawson said wearily, 'John shot his father with a soft-nosed .308 bullet at the base of the pelvis. There's nothing left with which to entertain the girls. And with Swanby dead and his father dying, we might very well be taking on a Duke ourselves when John arrives.'

'Jesus!' Kyle made way for a trooper in body armour and mask who pushed past, his rifle held at the ready.

'I'll go in. Luck, Sir.'

'The same to you,' Dawson said seriously. 'I'm beginning to think we might need it.'

John Willoughby had reached Belgravia without incident, pushing the Zed-Force Bedford to its limit, and had parked alongside a cluster of similar trucks no more than fifty yards from Steele's front door. The area was cordoned off with ropes and patrolled by police with dogs but he unhurriedly ducked the rope and said to the nearest P.C., 'Keep that brute off me, I've got a message for the Colonel.'

He waddled awkwardly towards the house, actually pushing past Kyle whom he recognised but ignored. John Willoughby had remembered the pantry window.

At the back of the house there was less light and noise, but there were two alert Zed-Force men standing a yard or two from the window. They were wearing their armour but not the headgear.

' 'Ello, chum.' The bigger of the two was a corporal. 'Come to relieve me?'

'I've come to relieve both of you,' John said. 'The Colonel says he'd like you to have a nice rest.' He was holding the rifle across his body with both hands, the muzzle pointing downwards. As the men began to grin he swung the stock in a short tight arc against the corporal's temple, then backhanded the trooper viciously in the same manner. The troopers toppled almost in unison.

Breathing quickly but evenly, he dragged the two bodies one after the other into the deeper shadows and then returned to the window.

The pantry light was on – the whole house was ablaze with lights although all curtains had been drawn – but the distorted view through the frosted glass indicated no movement and John was satisfied that both pantry and kitchen were empty.

It was easy to distinguish the pane that had replaced the broken one because the putty holding it in place was still white and soft. With difficulty John extracted a knife from his pocket and began to strip away the putty which gave easily under the sharp edge, so that in moments the glass was only lodged in position. As he moved the tip of his knife forward to insert it on one side and ease it out, it fell on to his gloved hand of its own accord.

John put the pane down carefully, then reached inside, pulled down the catch and opened the window silently.

Within two minutes he was inside Jack Steele's house.

There was a two-way radio set on a table in the lounge and Steele, Colonel Colin Campbell, Bingham-Pope and a recently-returned Kyle were standing by it.

'I'm sure my lads at Road-block No. 1 will get him,' Campbell was saying. 'Depending upon what speed he was travelling, they should be coming in any moment now.'

The set squawked and a garbled voice said, 'Lieutenant Malcolm to Colonel Sir. Over.'

'Receiving. Over.' Campbell barked.

'Road-block No. 1 shot up, Colonel Sir. All four lads killed. Truck and one uniform stolen. Sorry about this, sir. Over.'

'Ach, my poor wee laddies! Bairns, just. I'll get him for this! All right, Malcolm, it wasna your fault. Check with the other road blocks to see whether they let through one of our Bedfords containg a driver on his own. Over.'

'Wilco, Colonel Sir. Over and out.'

'Well, Kyle.' Steele looked at the policeman with sardonically raised eyebrows. 'This young man is proving not only far more difficult to apprehend than you anticipated, but bloody ruthless as well.'

'He's a hunter.' Kyle went over to a table and poured himself a drink. 'He's matched his cunning with the big cats. He's a dead shot. He's a born killer, really. It's just that this is the first time he's tried his hand with humans.' He regarded the amber liquid in the glass. 'How have you distributed your people?'

'I put Careless and Charles on the top floor. They've got Tim's cannon and one of your Walthers. Michael Jenkins and Hansom are on the office floor, which also contains storage rooms and so on. Clarke is here on the ground floor and Holland is roving wherever the blazes he wishes.'

Kyle put his glass down so suddenly that it rang and whisky slopped over the edge. 'Colonel, are your men ever armed with rifles?'

'Never, they're useless for our close-quarter work. I . . .'

'Would a man be allowed to use his own weapon on duty?'

'No.' The Scotsman's eyes narrowed. 'What are you getting at, Kyle?'

'While I was outside a trooper pushed past me. He was in body armour and gas mask and he was carrying a *rifle*, one of those odd-looking autoloaders with a pistol grip as well as a stock. Cetme-Sports, I think they're called.'

Campbell said urgently, 'That's not one of my men!'

'Then I think Willoughby has arrived,' Kyle said into the silence.

The radio squawked. 'Malcolm to Colonel Sir. Over.'

'Receiving, over.'

'All road blocks report letting through a Zed-Force Bedford with a single driver. I think that's him, sir. Over.'

'It's him all right. Tighten up outside. Every man of my Force is to identify himself. If he's wearing headgear he must remove it. Put it over the loudhailer. Oh, and Malcolm, send some lads around the back. Over.'

Kyle suddenly said, 'God, that pantry window, have you got somebody watching . . .'

The lights went off.

Because of the heavy curtains it was utterly dark throughout the big old house. Calls went up from the men on different floors. Campbell threw himself to the floor and bumped Steele. He whispered, 'Don't say a word for God's sake. Kyle and I will take the chances.'

Again the radio squawked, much louder now in the darkness. 'Colonel, is that a normal power failure you've got or is he there? Over.' There was only a fraction of a second's pause and then the astute Lieutenant's voice returned. 'Don't answer, sir, you'll make a sitting target. I'll wait for the men who checked the back.' There was a pause, then, 'Here they come. Our two fellows are unconscious, sir. Pantry window forced and wide open. He's in there. I'm not going to send in any more men because we'll end up shooting at each other. If you agree, then *don't* answer. We're going to try and rig up some emergency lighting which we'll get in to you.'

Campbell whispered with his lips an inch from Steele's ear, 'He's right. Who's your best man with the fuse-board?'

'Clarke. I'll get him.'

'No! Mon, I swear I'll slug ye if ye take risks.' Campbell suddenly shouted, 'Clarke, make your way here but don't answer!'

There was the blast of three shots and the radio set jangled. Both Kyle and Campbell fired back. Silence returned to their ringing eardrums.

'Anybody hurt?' The whisper barely floated to Kyle.

'No.' He wriggled across the floor and put his lips right against Campbell's ear. 'Willoughby doesn't know the General is in this room. We weren't talking much and he was at the fuse-board which is in the kitchen, so he couldn't have heard our voices. I'm going to try and tempt Willoughby upstairs.'

'That's a guid idea as long as ye realize ye might get shot. All right, Kyle.'

There was a rustle and Clarke's whisper sounded. 'Sir?'

'Do you think you can get the lights going again?'

'Depends upon what he's done, sir. He might have just tripped the main. But he might also have pulled the fuses out and put them somewhere. I'll try, sir.' He wriggled away with hardly a murmur of his departure.

Campbell conveyed Kyle's idea to Steele, who agreed. The the three of them wormed their way towards the shelter of the sofa, from where Kyle shouted suddenly, 'General, stay up there and don't move! Don't make a sound! Just stay there!'

Again their ears were blasted by a succession of shots. The window above their heads shattered and a soft-nosed slug gourged into the arm of the sofa. They did not fire back this time.

A long silence settled, broken by a quick rattle of shots on the stairs and then Jenkins's high excited voice, 'Colonel, he passed me on the stairs! I swear it! We had a go and I think I nicked him but I'm not sure.'

From high above came Careless's bull-like roar. 'It's okay, we've got the General in the billiard room and we won't let nobody in!'

'Bloody fool!' Steele began, then chuckled. 'I owe Careless an apology, he's smarter than I thought. Keep up the act, Kyle!'

'Careless shut up, you ass!' Kyle screamed.

'Everybody out,' Campbell breathed. 'Not you, sir, you stay right where you are. Come on, Kyle, we've moved him up.'

They felt their way to the stairs and began a slow and careful ascent until they heard the sound of muted breathing.

'It's me.' Jenkins moved slightly.

'Good lad. Go down and join the General just in case we've been out-smarted.'

'The General's right behind you. I've just bumped into him.'

'God, Steele!' Kyle snarled. 'Get back down there!'

'And let you act like a bunch of nursemaids? Not a chance.'

There was a short, whispered argument which Steele won, and they went on, passing the first floor and stopping on the landing of the second. A spurt of flame came from the far darkness and bullets chipped the plaster above their heads. Then the same weapon fired again but in a different direction. From the den came the sound of a groan and then a body falling.

'He will go through to check.' Kyle crouched against the wall. 'Someone definitely was hit and he thinks it's the General. All right, come along now!'

They went quickly but quietly down the blacked out passage until a whisper stopped them at the door of the billiard room.

'On the floor. He's been firing high.'

Campbell and Kyle inched their way into the room on their bellies. There was no sound at all and the darkness was total. Everyone was playing a waiting game.

Then the lights came on.

Kyle was furthest into the room. In the sudden shocking glare he saw John Willoughby at the far end, standing with his back against the fireplace, his rifle held across his chest, wearing only the Zed-Force tunic and trousers. No more than six yards away, Holland was coming painfully to his knees, his big Magnum swinging up. There was blood on his waist.

Willoughby was lost for a target. Then he saw Steele in the doorway and swung the rifle around but it was still moving when Holland's Magnum boomed and a red flower blossomed on John's chest. Only his reflexes squeezed the trigger once more and the bullet sliced its way down the middle of the billiard table's baize.

As the young man slid to the floor Holland was grinning, bringing the Magnum around until it pointed directly at

Steele. But before he could fire, a gun banged deafeningly from the doorway and Holland's head turned into a bloody spray of bone and matter and he collapsed on the tiled floor.

In the deathly hush that followed, Careless's voice said calmly, while smoke still trickled from the muzzle of his old Webley, 'That'll teach him to kick me in the balls.'

XVIII

Sir Howard Fuller, doyen of Britain's psychiatrists and code-named Uncle by the Special Branch, was holding a news conference in the drawing-room of Jack Steele's house in Belgravia. Extra chairs had been brought in and every major newspaper in the country was represented by a senior man or woman. Cameras flashed and television equipment created havoc on both sides of the big room.

Seated with Sir Howard at a table were Jack Steele, Colin Campbell, Charles Bingham-Pope and Assistant Commissioner Dawson. The shooting of a young lord, especially one who had made allegations of a sensational nature, needed thorough explanation and this was the reason for their presence. The original diary lay in front of Sir Howard Fuller and each representative of the Press had been given a photocopy and allowed to study it before the conference had begun.

Fuller said, 'I think I have explained the medical side of it pretty fully, tracing Lord John Willoughby's progressive deterioration by the entries in his diary. I have also given you some other case histories of genuine patients to enable you to make comparisons. It is now question time.'

A wintry-looking woman in tweeds immediately asked waspishly, 'The wildest rumours have been circulating about Lady Mary Willoughby's part in this sordid affair. She certainly departed for Spain in a hurry. Where does she fit into the picture?'

Dawson shifted in his chair. 'We are not sure. It seems that she might have played a small part in egging her brother on for reasons unknown to us other than pure guesswork. We feel in other words that she was taken in by her brother and believed in his "Protector Conclusion".' He did not add that, with the villain having fled, both Lomax and Greer had been released and Kyle had resigned. He had broken every rule in the book by allowing Mary Willoughby to leave, and thus had very little option. He would shortly be winging his way to Ottowa to visit an old friend, Hal Turner of the R.C.M.P., with a view to joining that force. Without him to tie the ends together, there would be insufficient evidence against Greer and Lomax, and here again the L.M.P. had no alternative but to let them go.

Brent of *The Times* asked dryly, 'Just one more thing on paranoiacs. Are they always as difficult to detect as Willoughby?'

'Not necessarily.' Uncle sipped at a glass of water. 'Sometimes their delusions are so bizarre that it is obvious they are mentally ill, even to a layman. Lord John was difficult, as I have already stated, because I was working entirely from diary entries without having had a chance to examine the man, besides which he was the textbook portrait of a suspicious and deluded person whose general behaviour *apart* from his delusion demonstrated a high intelligence and social acceptability.'

An American voice asked, 'Mr Steele, Lord John's initial suspicions were based on two things: the military nature of your household and a visit by Colonel Campbell. Could you throw some light on this please?'

Steele smiled. 'I was a soldier for many years. I made and cemented many friendships which I see no reason to break. My desire to enter politics was motivated entirely by a wish to do my part in getting this country on its feet again. Most professional soldiers are efficient organizers, so I asked – or persuaded if you like – Mr Bingham-Pope and Mr Hansom to join me. Michael Jenkins approached *me* for a position, and when he told me that he had served in the Parachute Regiment I will admit that I was influenced. He is a tough, calm, and efficient young man. As for Careless and Clarke, they had served me so well that I couldn't abandon them to the vagaries of the army. Apart from that, they too had become my friends.' That small, curving smile appeared. 'Colonel Campbell will answer the other half of your question.'

Campbell said ruefully, 'I was sent for by Mr Steele who demanded to know whether the rumour about the Garment Workers' demonstration was true. In other words, whether I had rigged it. I denied this but he nevertheless gave me a general but thorough ticking off, warning me to keep my nose out of his affairs.'

There was a little laughter. A roly-poly man said, 'Is it true that you were born in the same village as Oliver Cromwell?'

Steele studied him solemnly. 'Yes it is, but I had no say in it.'

This time they laughed. The *Mirror* representative asked, 'Where have you hidden your Field Marshal's uniform?'

More laughter, into which Steele smilingly said, 'With my full knowledge and co-operation, two of the major newspapers of this country have checked every military tailor in existence and drawn a blank. Apart from which I cannot think of a worse fate than to be a Field Marshal.'

The man from the *Daily Worker* jumped to his feet, which put him five feet one inch above the floor. 'Is it not a fact that you brought about the so-called "Cricketpitch Conference" by blackmailing Joe Mullins with pictures taken of him with a woman by the name of Irma Saler?'

Steele's mood changed. He glowered at the reporter. 'You are here on sufferance, little man; I don't like that word "blackmail". If I had a hold on him because of dirty pictures then how could he have turned me down flat?'

There was a murmur of agreement. Somebody asked, 'Does the 74th Field Regiment really have a tradition going back to Cromwell, and do they propose a toast as described in Lord John's diary? Or was that an hallucination too?

No, it wasn't. Otherwise the answer is in the affirmative all round. There are many strange traditions in old Regiments of the Line. I approve of them, even if some seem silly to civilians, because they are good for morale.'

A grave-looking man said, 'Lord John was puzzled about the fact that you had two sets of telephone numbers and frankly so am I. Why was this?'

Steele said, 'Because those in the back of my appointment book were friends. There are many high-ranking officers amongst them because I rubbed shoulders with these men for twenty years. But there are men from other walks of life, including a member of the Fourth Estate.'

He was referring to Tony North of *The Times* and there was again general laughter. The group stirred. Already their minds were working ahead to how they would word their stories.

'Any more questions?' Sir Howard Fuller asked.

There was a general shaking of heads. Steele stood up. 'Thank you for coming, ladies and gentlemen. Before you go I would like to say one more thing, which is that I liked John Willoughby and mourn his passing. There was much in him that was fine. From the psychiatric evidence you have heard, I think that the blame for his tragic life and death may be placed not on him but firmly at the doorstep of a certain old man who lies dying in hospital. Thank you.'

That night the headlines of the *Standard* screamed: MAD DUKE'S SON DIES FOR NOTHING.

Only Kyle and Dawson attended the funeral of Lord John Willoughby which was held an hour or two after the press conference.

EPILOGUE

Extract from Gird me with Steele *by Charles Bingham-Pope, page 321*

There was a round dozen of us in Steele's study, including Steele himself, General Fitzmaurice, Brigadier Howard, Air Commodore Judson, Colonel Colin Campbell, Rear Admiral Worth, Jenkins, Hansom and myself. All of us, with the exception of those in the navy, were in full battledress, and none of us moved. I remember noting at the time how still we were, not a sound spoken, every man with his eyes glued to his watch. There was not one of us who did not jump when the telephone rang and Campbell snatched it up.

He spoke very briefly. Then he replaced the receiver and said, 'My men are in position, sir. No incidents.'

Steele said firmly, 'You must make it very clear to your men, Colin, that any members deciding to evacuate either House, which some will no doubt do, must be treated extremely courteously and taken straight to the temporary concentration camp in St James's Park, aside from those who may immediately declare to throw in their lot with us. Now, what about the Guards?'

'They are agreeable to our use of the Palace.'

Steele grunted. 'Thank God, that helps.' He checked his watch yet again. 'It's time.' He stretched out and picked up the red telephone, waited a moment then said, 'Philip? Now

hear this. *Turn the guns on London.* I repeat. *Turn the guns on London.*'

There was another silence into which only the faint sound of the telephone being replaced intruded. Then Steele smiled. 'I wonder what young John would say if he were able to know that he came to the right conclusion for the wrong reasons?'

He began to chuckle. 'Poor little bastard. If only he knew!' The rest of us became infected, and out of their tension those dozen grown men, myself included, howled with laughter until our sides ached while Careless and Clarke, entering in full uniform with F.N.s slung over their shoulders, stared at us in amazement. Then someone began to sing, 'There'll always be an England', and one by one the rest of us joined in:

> *And England shall be free,*
> *If England means as much to you,*
> *As England means to me*

They were still singing when the transports roared up out of the darkness to take us to the half-dozen or more different control points where we would be needed, and to take people like Fitzmaurice, Judson and Howard back to their commands which were busy at that moment forming a ring of steel about London.

I went with Jack Steele directly to the Palace, from which he would deliver his ultimatum to Parliament and then address the nation.